REBEL
of the
Lazy H Ranch

REBEL
of the
Lazy H Ranch

Bernard Palmer

ACCENT BOOKS
Denver, Colorado

Second Printing 1980
Third Printing 1981

ACCENT BOOKS
A division of Accent Publications, Inc.
12100 W. Sixth Avenue
P.O. Box 15337
Denver, Colorado 80215

Library of Congress Catalog Card Number: 79-53566

ISBN 0-89636-033-4

1.

Greg Powell scrunched lower in the pickup seat and squinted through the side window. A thin layer of clouds spider-webbed the blue sky, dimming the forces of the morning sun. The way it looked now, the snow wasn't going to melt much that morning.

He pushed his wide-brimmed hat back on his head and frowned his impatience. That was one of the problems of being 14 years old. It took forever for things to happen.

In the fall he had waited impatiently for the first snow so he and Hipolita Rodriguez, who lived across the street, could go tobogganing or try their luck skiing on the short eastern Colorado hills. Then he and Hip had waited for Christmas to come creeping in, one ponderous, slow-moving day at a time.

Now he was waiting for the sun as it inched south in anticipation of the coming spring. It had already been at work. Bare spots on the recently white sage-choked hills were robbing the boys of their ski run. Still, it wasn't quite warm enough for them to saddle their horses and shake out their lariats to practice their favorite sport, roping.

Greg and Hip were stuck like sailors on a calm sea, in one of those impossible periods of the year when time remained motionless and there was nothing to do that was any fun.

"I sure wish I could have brought Hip along," he muttered to no one in particular as his dad pulled out onto the highway and passed the sign that marked the city limits on their way to the Lazy H Ranch.

Had Greg turned in the seat or looked out the rearview mirror he could have read the legend: *CONCORD, POPULATION 1627.* But he didn't have to. He had seen it hundreds of times. He knew every bullet hole in the board and every fleck of chipped paint. He even knew the guys who had attempted to demonstrate their sense of humor by penciling in two zeroes and a comma to the population figure.

"I sure wish Hip could have gone with us," he repeated.

His sister Kimberly turned from her place in the seat beside him and made a face, the freckles on her nose crinkling. "There isn't room."

"There would've been if you'd stayed at home with Kevin and Mom."

"Only I didn't stay home," she continued triumphantly. "I'm going out to the Lazy H because Daddy asked me to."

"We could have taken the station wagon," George Powell said, "but when I phoned Mr. Huffman he asked me to bring you two."

"He did?" Greg exclaimed.

His dad nodded. "And the way he said it, I figured he didn't want anyone else. He's concerned about that nephew of his who's living with him now. He'd like to have him make some friends."

"I know that nephew of his," Greg said curtly.

Bernard Palmer

"He's in my class at school."

"So, we're elected," Kim said. "Is that it?"

Mr. Powell cast a quick glance in her direction. "I'm surprised at you, Kim."

"You wouldn't say that if you knew Frank Ellis, Daddy. He—he's *gross!*"

Her dad glanced at the odometer to be sure he didn't pass the turn-off to the Lazy H. "As I understand it, he's a confused, badly hurt boy who hasn't been able to make many friends since he left Illinois."

"There's a reason for that," she countered. "He swears and says dirty things and lies and—and he tries to bully the kids who are littler than he is." She shuddered. "No one at school can stand him."

"Perhaps that's his way of telling us how badly he's hurt and how much he needs friends."

Greg turned slightly to look at his sister who was sitting in the middle on a pillow to allow her to see over the pickup hood. Although she was 12 years old she was shorter than anyone else in her seventh grade class, slender as a sunflower stalk and with a smile that reminded him of the bright yellow summer flower. Kim always made him think of summer.

Greg again turned his attention out the window to the hills. A small herd of antelope had been feeding on the sparse, dry grass until the sound of the pickup attracted their attention. Now they were staring curiously in the direction of the road.

Greg could understand how Frank must feel

8

at having to leave his parents and all his friends and go 900 miles away to a place where he didn't know anyone except an aunt and an uncle. It must be tough for him.

"Why would he have to come way out here to school?"

Mr. Powell tightened his grip on the wheel. "You remember how it was a few years ago with Hipolita, don't you?"

"You mean when his dad was drinking so much and left home?" He remembered all right. That was before the Rodriguez family started going to church and became Christians.

"Frank's folks are having the same kind of trouble," George Powell went on. "Only they're getting a divorce and neither of them thought they could take him and care for him. That's why he's out here living with Lee Huffman and his wife."

Greg studied the distant hills once more. That did make things a little different, he realized. His own parents seldom even had a disagreement and he'd never known them to get really mad at each other.

"That's heavy," he murmured.

George Powell turned off the main road, drove past one ranch and was now heading for the Lazy H. For several minutes Greg had been studying the ranch buildings a couple of miles away. They were set neatly at the end of a winding, treeless lane that skirted a steep hill, curved around a ravine and climbed a long slope to a plateau overlooking the valley to the west.

Bernard Palmer

The huge barn dominated the scene. It was a towering white, hip-roofed structure with a white plank corral at the back and a cluster of gleaming, well-painted granaries, machine sheds, a blacksmith shop and two silos arranged at the sides and along the front.

The house of white brick was the only building on the ranch not intimidated by the barn. It stood apart from the other structures, a proud old dowager with her head held high. A wide chimney on one side marked the location of the fireplace and a long thermopane window commanded a panoramic view of the hills.

As they came to a stop, Greg's eyes widened and he pulled himself erect.

"Wow!" he exclaimed. "Look, Dad! There are rodeo chutes on the other side of the corral and bleachers and everything. Man! They've got a bigger and better setup out here than there is at the fairgrounds in town."

"Why else would you think this year's Colorado Little Mavericks' Rodeo would be held out here?"

Greg's eyes widened still further, if that were possible. The Little Mavericks' Rodeo was just about the biggest event held for kids in the ranch country of the state. Riders and ropers from all over flocked to compete in it and the winners got to go on to the National Rodeo.

"Is that what you're going to be photographing out here for *Western World*?" he asked. It still didn't seem real that the big event would be held so close to Concord.

"Why didn't you tell us?" Kim demanded.

Her dad laughed. "I told you."

"You know what I mean."

Greg breathed deeply. "Do you suppose Hip and I could enter the breakaway calf roping and goat tying and maybe the calf riding?"

"And me?" Kim put in. "I'm real good at barrel racing. Can I enter that event, Dad?"

"We'll have to see about that a little later," Mr. Powell said.

There was no one in the yard, but the Huffmans must have been watching from the house. The instant the Powell pickup stopped, a lean, gray-haired man came out the kitchen door, wriggling into a sheepskin coat. Frank Ellis followed a couple of steps behind. He was still wearing those expensive new boots he had been bragging to Greg about at school. And he had on a new cowboy hat that hid his black hair. He was shorter than Greg by half a head, and as dark as the blond boy in the truck was fair.

A surly scowl marred Frank's handsome features and he swaggered when he walked. "I don't like you and I don't care who knows it," his manner shouted.

"Howdy, George," Lee Huffman said, extending a great, bear-like paw. "Come on in and sit a spell. Then we'll go out and look over the arena. I've been fixin' it up a mite for the kids."

Greg and Kim got out of the pickup and looked around. Frank had stopped several paces from them and was surveying them arrogantly. "How come you brought *her* along?" he demanded, jerking his head in Kim's direction.

"He didn't bring me," she retorted. "Daddy did."

"Then why don't you go into the house with *Daddy?* We've got other things to do than play nursemaid to a stupid girl."

She wrinkled her face at him.

Quite deliberately Frank turned his back on Kim. "Do we *have* to have her with us everywhere we go? Can't you tell her to get lost?"

Greg's cheeks flushed and his fists clenched impulsively. He could get mad at Kim and argue with her, himself, but this was different. He wasn't about to let Frank shove her around. "I don't happen to want to," he said coldly.

Frank's eyes narrowed ominously and for an instant Greg was sure he was going to lip off again. If he did, there was going to be trouble.

However, Frank started toward the barn. "Want to see my new horse?"

2.

"I've got the best and fastest horse on the ranch," Frank boasted. "Uncle Lee gave me my pick." They climbed up on the corral fence and peered over the top railing at the horses that were milling restlessly inside the enclosure. "There he is! The red one."

"You mean the sorrel?" Greg asked.

"Sorrel?" He stared blankly at the Powell boy. "I—I—" He stopped, suddenly understanding what Greg meant. "Yeah, that's him. The sorrel. I call him Blaze."

Greg saw that the horse had good lines, but he was far from being the best horse on the ranch. He was older than the others in the corral by 10 or 12 years and had a slight stiffening in his legs that took some of the spring out of his proud step. And the deep sorrel color of his shaggy coat wore the frosted look of increasing age.

"Would you believe it?" Frank continued, "Blaze has won every quarter horse race he was ever entered in."

"He's a good-looking animal, all right."

"He can beat the pants off your horse," Frank challenged belligerently.

Greg looked away without answering.

"I'll prove it to you next Saturday. How about that?"

"No way. Patches is a roping horse and Kim rides him in barrel racing sometimes, but *I* don't race him."

A taunting smile marred Frank's face. "Scared you'll get beat?"

"No, he's not scared he'll get beat!" Kim burst out. "Patches could outrun that sorrel of yours on three legs."

"You'll have to prove that."

Anger flushed Greg's cheeks again. "We don't have to prove anything to you or anybody else."

"I suppose that's what you'll say about entering the Little Mavericks' Rodeo in May."

Greg shook his head. "As a matter of fact, Kim and I talked with Dad about it on the way out. We're both going to enter."

Frank's laughter was shrill and mocking. "You'd just as well save yourself the trouble. You'll never get anywhere."

"Maybe not." His jaw was set. "But we'll sure give it a try."

A sneer lifted one corner of the other boy's mouth. "You can save yourself the effort. I'm going to be entered, so you won't have a chance."

Greg faced him. "You?" he echoed.

"Want to lay a little bet that I won't beat you?"

"Where did you learn to rope?" Greg asked.

"Where do you suppose? Back in Illinois. People learn to ride and rope there, the same as they do here."

Greg didn't know much about Illinois but he had trouble believing that Frank Ellis had learned to ride and rope in Moline. After all, his home had been in the city. He didn't think anybody in a city would have a chance to learn to rope. They might have a few parks to ride in, but that was different.

"I won three ribbons with Rasputin—that's the name of my horse back in Illinois," Frank boasted. "I'd have brought him along when I had to come out here, but—" His voice trailed off.

"But what?"

A hurt that had been smoldering in his eyes moments before leaped into flame. For an instant Greg had the impression the boy was going to cry, but when Frank spoke his voice was harsh and empty of emotion.

"When Mom said that I—I had to come out here to live for awhile, Dad sold Rasputin. And he sold our house with the swimming pool, too."

Greg eyed him skeptically.

"You don't even think I can ride, do you?"

"I didn't say that," he retorted.

"Maybe you didn't say it, but I know what you think. I'm not that stupid." Anger and frustration honed Frank's voice.

Greg did not answer him.

Frank's lips trembled and his fists clenched in fury. "All right," he said, his words so taut they choked in his throat. "All right, if you don't believe me, I'll prove it to you. We'll go saddle up Blaze, or any other horse you want me to ride. I'll show you! And I'll show you I can rope, too."

Before Greg could reply his dad and Mr. Huffman came out into the yard, heading in the direction of the pickup.

Greg turned away but Frank grasped him by the arm. "Come back next Saturday," he said under his breath. "I'll prove to you that I can ride and rope as well as any guy on the ranch. OK?"

"Sorry. I don't think I can make it."

Frank said no more until the two men joined them. "Uncle Lee," he said quickly, "is it all right if Greg and Kim enter some of the events in the Little Mavericks' Rodeo?"

"It's fine with me if it's all right with their dad."

"We were talking about that on the way out. I think it's pretty well settled isn't it, kids?"

Greg hesitated. He had been so excited about entering the rodeo he hadn't even considered the fact that he and Hip didn't have a place where they could practice with real live calves and goats. Kim could go out to the fairgrounds and set up the barrels to practice for her event, but there was no way that he and his pal could sharpen their skills. A cold wave engulfed him. What was the use of entering the rodeo if he couldn't spend time practicing roping calves and tying goats. He voiced his concern to the others.

"No problem there," Lee Huffman said. "You and your friend can come and work out anytime you want to. And Kim, too. The boys can set up the barrels for you, Kim, and you can use the exact course we'll be using for the rodeo." He paused. "How about it?"

She hesitated for a moment.

"You'll have the advantage over most of the other entries if you do that," he reminded her. "You'll be familiar with the course."

Bernard Palmer

She turned to her father. "What do you think, Daddy?"

"Like I said, it's all right with me."

"Then it's all settled," Mr. Huffman put in.

"Hey, that's neat!" Frank exclaimed.

"Bring the kids out the first Saturday the weather's fit. OK, George?"

"I don't know why not."

Mr. Powell got into the pickup and rolled down the window. The rancher leaned against it. He offered to loan them a horse trailer to transport their horses out to the ranch, but the Powells already had a horse trailer.

"When you come back for the kids Saturday afternoon, George," Lee said, smiling warmly, "I should have some more dope on the rodeo. The entries are already beginning to come in."

"Sounds good."

"Come early enough so we can chat for awhile and have a couple of drinks. OK?"

"The chatting sounds fine," Mr. Powell said casually, "but I'll have to pass on the drinks."

Concern gleamed in the older man's eyes. "Have a problem with it?" he asked, lowering his voice. "I know what that is. Never had it myself, but liquor caused most of the trouble between my sister and her husband. Frank's parents. My brother-in-law couldn't handle it."

"No," George Powell answered, shaking his head. "I've never had any trouble with liquor. I've never used it."

The rancher scratched his ear with his forefinger. "How come?"

"Well, in high school I was into athletics and

18

didn't want to break training," he said. "And when I went to college it was on a football scholarship. I didn't drink then, either, because of training rules. I figured I had to take care of myself if I was going to play well. Then, before I graduated from college, I was introduced to Jesus Christ and received Him as my Saviour. What I read in the Bible convinces me that it's best for a Christian not to drink, so I don't. It's as simple as that."

Lee shook his head incredulously. "A Jesus freak. If I hadn't heard it from you, George, I'd never have believed it." He pulled in a deep breath. "I've never held much with religion myself, but when you come out I'll see if we can't stir up some coffee for us. OK?"

"Sounds good."

"Then it's all settled. We'll see the three of you next Saturday." He glanced in Greg's direction. "You can bring that friend of yours along, too, if you want to."

Greg thanked him and got into the pickup beside his sister. Mr. Powell started the engine, waved to the ranch owner and his nephew and backed around to head out the lane.

3.

Bernard Palmer

After dinner that evening the subject of the Little Mavericks' Rodeo came up again. Ten-year-old Kevin had heard his folks talk about it but only in relation to the photo story his dad was doing. He knew very little about what took place at such a contest and neither did his mother. She asked about it curiously.

"It's neat, Mom," Greg said. He was still thrilled by the prospect of competing in a real, live rodeo. "They have most of the events a regular rodeo does, only they change some of them. Instead of calf roping and tying they have goat tying and breakaway roping for both boys and girls. And they have bronc riding and barrel racing and lots of other things."

"That sounds super," Kevin broke in.

"There'll be real rodeo officials and contestants from all over the state. The winners will get to go to Cheyenne to the National Little Mavericks' Rodeo. Isn't that great?"

"Yeah, it sure is," Kevin said, excitement and envy dancing in his blue eyes. That's for me!"

"You?" Kim echoed. "Are you out of your mind?"

He wrinkled his face at her. "How about it, Dad? Can I enter the rodeo, too? Can I?"

"What would you enter?" Greg exclaimed.

He thought for a moment. "I could enter lots of things," he said lamely, "if I wanted to."

22

"Like what?" his older brother persisted.

"Like bull riding," he blurted.

Mrs. Powell looked up, disapproval written in her usually pleasant features. She acted as though she was about to speak but Greg cut her off.

"You riding a bull?" he exploded. "You'd be scared to get within 200 yards of a bull. Don't make me laugh!"

"You just wait!" the younger boy boasted defensively. "I'll show you! I'll enter the bull riding and—"

"Guys your age won't be riding any bulls," Greg corrected. "They use tame little calves for the Junior Calf Riding."

"There won't be any bull riding for you, young man," Mrs. Powell broke in firmly. "Or calf riding, either. So you can just forget entering that event. We aren't going to have you in the hospital with a broken head or arm or leg if we can help it."

Kevin turned to his dad, his eyes pleading desperately for support. "It's all right if I enter the bull—I mean the calf-riding, isn't it, Dad?" When the answer did not come immediately, he continued, "I won't get hurt. Honest I won't."

"I know you won't get hurt by a bucking calf," his mother retorted in a tone that meant the conversation had gone far enough. "You're not going to be riding any."

"I don't know why not," he argued still. "I can ride as well as Kim any day."

Kim bristled slightly, "That," she exclaimed, "I would have to see."

"She isn't going to be riding any calves, either."

"But, Mom!" Kevin protested again, "I could win here and go on to the national championship rodeo in Cheyenne."

He pulled himself erect. "I'd probably win there, too. Kevin Powell, National Little Mavericks' Rodeo calf riding champion, junior division. How does that grab you?"

His mother smiled crookedly. "I'd rather have you plain, ordinary Kevin Powell in one piece—without any broken bones or bandages."

"OK," he grumbled, "but it'll probably ruin my whole life."

Mr. Powell broke up the conversation at that point by suggesting that they all go in the other room and play Monopoly. It was a spirited game and before long the Little Mavericks' Rodeo, Frank Ellis and his uncle were completely forgotten. But only for a time.

The next morning Greg phoned the Rodriguez home and talked to his best friend, Hip. He had something exciting to tell him, he said, and wanted to know if he could be at Sunday school a bit early.

"I'm always there early," Hip reminded him. "You know that. I go to help Dad get the classrooms ready."

Everybody, including Greg, knew that Mr. Rodriguez was the janitor at the church and had been since his conversion almost four years before. He had volunteered for the job when they had difficulty getting someone to do it and had been faithful ever since.

"Yeah," Greg said. "I know you're at church early. I mean, could you meet me out front a few minutes before the bell? I've got something to talk to you about."

"Sounds exciting."

"You'll be there?"

"Sure thing!"

The Powell family wasn't ready for Sunday school soon enough to suit Greg so he rode his bike down the wide, tree-lined street to the church. He was just riding up the walk when Hip came out the front door to look for him.

"Hi, Greg!" The youthful Chicano came down the steps. "What's this all about?" he asked, taking the handlebars of Greg's bike as his friend rode up and stopped.

"We were out to the Lazy H Ranch yesterday," Greg began.

"And Mr. Huffman told you about the kids' rodeo that's going to be held there in May. Is that it?"

Greg's eyelids widened in surprise. "How did you know?"

"He phoned Dad yesterday afternoon," Hip went on. "He wants him to help handle the rodeo stock. They're bringing in some horses and calves and goats from a ranch near Laramie."

"Isn't it exciting?" Greg exclaimed. "We'll have a chance to win the right to go to the national championships."

"What do you mean? Mr. Huffman didn't ask for me to come along, did he?"

Greg drew in a long breath. "Well, he said I

Bernard Palmer

could bring a friend."

That didn't satisfy Hip. "Does he know that I'm your friend?" he persisted. "Did you tell him that your best pal's a Chicano?"

"That wouldn't make any difference."

"That's what *you* think! You and your family aren't the same as a lot of the people around here," he continued, his lips trembling bitterly. "We're treated like scum by some of them."

Greg felt his temper rise at the thought that there were people in Concord who treated Hip and his family as though they didn't amount to anything because they weren't white.

"Besides," his friend added, "how're you and I going to get good enough to win anything? The guys on the ranches'll have real live calves and goats to work out with. We'll be lucky to get to practice with real animals once or twice before the rodeo. We're beat before we start."

"I wouldn't say that," Greg countered, his grin broadening. "It just so happens that Mr. Lee Huffman gave us a special invitation to come out anytime we want to, to work out. He's got lots of goats and calves we can practice with. He'll even have one of the hands get 'em in the chute for us."

Hip frowned suspiciously. "What's the catch?"

"Catch?" Greg echoed. "What catch?"

"There's got to be some kind of a gimmick to a fantastic deal like that. What does he expect of us in return?"

"Nothing." Greg expelled his breath slowly. "Nothing. Only—"

"Only what?"

"He asked Dad if we'd be nice to Frank Ellis."

Hip groaned.

"That's the way I felt 'til I got to thinking about it. We've got a good deal."

Hip relaxed his grip on the handlebars of his friend's bike and turned for a moment to stare off across the vacant lot next to the church building. "Maybe," he said doubtfully.

"We've been praying and praying that God would provide us some calves and goats to work out with. Now He's done it. We ought to thank Him for that."

Hip nodded his agreement. "I guess you're right but I sure didn't think He would answer by giving us a guy like Frank to associate with."

Greg expected Frank Ellis to be as arrogant at school on Monday morning as he had been at the ranch on Saturday, and in some ways he was as haughty and contemptuous as ever. But in others there was a softness about him; a loneliness, a bewilderment that seemed to cry out to those around him. He swaggered through the halls intimidating anyone who would not stand up to him; but even as he did so, the hurt gleamed in his eyes.

At times Greg Powell noticed the other boy's shoulders sag and the strength seemed to flee from his thin young frame. Seeing the confusion and pain in Frank's features, Greg's heart went out to him, in spite of himself. Greg could not even imagine how he would feel if his mother and dad separated and were getting a divorce. He was glad that he didn't have to

Bernard Palmer

worry about anything like that.

Greg and Hip were having lunch in the school cafeteria Monday noon when Frank Ellis came over and confidently sat down at the table across from them, as though they were now his special friends.

"Did you talk to Hip about coming out to the ranch on Saturdays to practice roping?"

Greg nodded.

"Yeah, we talked about it this morning," the dark-skinned Chicano put in.

Frank turned to face Hip, who was an inch or two shorter than he was. "Well how about it? Are you coming or aren't you?"

Greg thought he detected a certain belligerence in the newcomer's voice, but he could not be sure.

"We'll be there," Hip replied. "Won't we, Greg?"

The Powell boy nodded. "I think we'll wait until the snow's gone, though. We don't want to risk running our horses until we're sure they'll have good footing."

"Your worries are about over. There's no snow in the corral now and hardly any in the pasture," Frank replied.

One corner of his mouth lifted into what was fast becoming a perpetual sneer as he continued. "You'd better get on with the practicing if you want to have a chance in the Little Mavericks' Rodeo."

He drew himself erect. "There's lots of competition already and, don't forget, you'll have to go up against me, too."

"Neato," Hip said, smiling easily.

"I suppose you're like everyone else around here and think I'm lousy because I'm not from the great West." He pulled in a deep breath. "I'll have you know that I'm just as good as you are."

"You won't get an argument out of me. If you can out-rope me or tie a goat faster than I can, I'm for you. I just do the best I can and don't worry about anyone else."

Frank's grin was tantalizing. "You're different than some guys around here that I know." With that he directed his hot gaze at Greg. "There are some people who don't think I can ride at all, but I'm goin' to show 'em."

Greg remained cool at the implied taunt.

"I'll tell you what, Greg. Bring your camera along and take pictures of me roping calves and tying goats. Then when you think you might want to make fun of me, you c'n take 'em out and look at 'em. That ought to stop you."

Greg Powell felt the color creep up his neck and spread along his cheeks. He didn't know why but Frank had the knack of making him feel inferior and defensive. He wanted to shout a denial, shout that he had never doubted the other boy's ability to ride well, but that would not have been the truth.

Grimly he faced Frank. "I've never said that you couldn't ride," he replied evenly, "but now that you mention it, I do wonder how you got to be as good as you say you are."

Frank's eyes flashed. "I'll show you," he retorted icily. "Just wait! I'll show you!"

"Now, wait a minute, both of you," Hip put in,

29

grinning. "I think I should warn you. I'm the best rider and roper in these parts. And if you don't believe that, just ask me. It won't take me long to tell you."

The laugh that followed seemed to ease the tension. Quite deliberately Frank got to his feet.

"I'll see you guys on Saturday," he murmured. He took a step or two toward the door before turning back. "And don't forget your camera, Powell! I'm goin' to give you some pictures you won't want to miss!" With that he swaggered away.

A minute passed and neither Greg nor Hipolita spoke. Then Greg put both hands on the table, palms down, as though he was about to push himself to his feet. "That guy!" he exploded. "Did you ever see anyone like him?"

"I've seen worse," Hip said mildly.

"Well I haven't! And Dad expects me to be nice to him!"

The rest of the week the weather stayed cold and there was little melting anywhere. The drifts seemed to get dirtier and the crust on top of them harder, but that was all. They certainly didn't seem to be any smaller.

At first the boys talked about getting Mr. Powell to take them out to the Lazy H but decided against it, in spite of what Frank had said about the snow being gone from the corral. They elected to give the ground another week or so to thaw and dry out.

That morning they cleaned out the barn where they kept their horses and the spindling three-year-old, Sawdust, that George Powell had bought for Kim the fall before. It was almost noon when they finished.

While they were working, Kim rode out to the fairgrounds on her bike and came back to report that the snow out there was gone and the ground didn't seem to be frozen. She thought it was dry enough for them to ride in the arena.

"Hey, that's neat!" Hip exclaimed.

"Maybe we should've gone out to the Lazy H this morning, after all," observed Greg, reluctantly.

That afternoon the boys and Kim saddled their horses and rode across town to the fairgrounds. It had been several weeks since their horses had been saddled and they were high-spirited. Especially Kimberly's young horse. Sawdust had been well-broken before she got him and was as gentle as any good gelding his age, but he was in top condition and spoiling to run. He fiddle-footed along the back alley, fighting the reins and the bit in his mouth.

"Be careful, Kim," Hip warned. "He acts like he wants to get out and go."

She tightened the grip of her knees on Sawdust's withers and pulled his head even higher to let him know he would be fighting the bit in his mouth if he should bolt. Her movements were gentle, but strong and positive. Sawdust had to know that she was the master of the situation and that he had to obey her.

Greg watched her proudly. One thing he had to say about that vivacious sister of his: She not only loved horses, she knew how to handle

Bernard Palmer

them. There was no doubt that she could ride anything he could.

At the fairgrounds they checked the area carefully, then gave the horses their heads and let them run until their sides were heaving and their withers were moist with sweat.

When they stopped, their mounts were content to stand, breathing heavily.

Greg and Hip got the barrels and set them up while Kim checked her saddle to be sure the cinch was tight.

"We're all set if you are," her brother called out.

She mounted and took a firm grip on the reins.

"Want us to time you?"

"Not today, I've got to let Sawdust get the feel of what we're doing. It has been a long time since he has run the barrels."

With that she galloped him across the arena, around the first barrel and over to the second. Although she tried desperately to guide him through the cloverleaf, he hit the second barrel with his shoulder and sent it rolling. It was the same with the third.

She tried again after the boys set the barrels back in place, but this time Sawdust shied as he approached the first and it was all she could do to keep him from bolting. She had to kick him in the flanks with her heels and saw on the reins to get him to go around it. The skin on his neck quivered nervously and his eyes were wide and staring.

"He acts to me as though he's afraid of them," Hip said.

"I'll try him again." She gritted her teeth and brought the frightened young horse around once more.

"Want me to try him for you?" Greg asked.

She shook her head. "I'm the one who's going to be racing him. He has got to learn from me."

4.

Kimberly was so concerned about training Sawdust that she rushed home after school every night the following week, saddled and rode him over to the fairgrounds where she worked him hard on the barrels. At first she walked him over the cloverleaf course, circling each barrel at the proper distance and letting him get the feel of what she expected of him. Then she urged him to a trot, making the same moves.

The young horse did as she wanted him to but for some reason Kim could feel the terror in her mount as he approached each successive barrel. The skin on his neck began to quiver nervously; his head came up and there was an almost imperceptible change in his stride—a hesitation that betrayed his fear.

"There now, Sawdust," she said, patting him reassuringly on the withers. "That's all right. They aren't going to hurt you."

After half a dozen trips over the course at a trot, she urged him to an easy, comfortable gallop. Approaching the first barrel, he fought the bit in a desperate though futile attempt to veer off. She managed to hold him but not before he swung wide in a great, time-eating circle.

The next time she braced herself in the stirrups and held the reins taut, sending him straight at the barrel. The maneuver seemed to cause him to come unglued. He fought for his head and broke stride, hitting the barrel with his shoulder, sending it rolling. But he approached the next barrel at a fast gallop and for one exhilarating instant Kim thought he had learned and was going to circle the barrel properly. Then, within half a dozen paces of it, he jerked to a halt in a puff of dust, so suddenly he almost threw Kim over his head. And for a moment both horse and rider remained motionless, trembling violently.

Kim wanted to leave the fairgrounds and go home immediately. She didn't think she dared ride Sawdust around the barrels again. Yet, from somewhere she remembered hearing an experienced horseman say that it was disastrous to stop working with an animal until he had done what the rider wanted him to do.

If Kim let him get away with disobeying once, she might ruin him. And she loved him too much for that. So she walked him to the starting line and began again. He didn't do very well, but after two or three tries she was able to get him around each of the barrels.

"All right, Sawdust," she murmured, patting him on the neck when they had circled the last barrel. "Let's go home."

It was almost six o'clock when she rode the young horse into the yard and stopped before the barn door. Greg, who had just finished feeding Patches, saw her coming. He realized there was something wrong by the sag of her shoulders and the dispirited way she sat her saddle.

"What's the matter?" he asked, grasping the bridle. "Have trouble again?"

She dismounted without answering him. He led the horse into the barn, took off the bridle and put the halter on before removing the saddle. Kim watched in silence.

"Want to tell me about it?" Greg asked at last.

"There's not much to tell. I just can't make Sawdust take the barrels. Not the way he should, anyway. I—I don't know what to do."

"Did you try shifting your weight to the inside stirrup and leaning in that direction as you rein him around the barrel?" Greg asked. He was sure she knew how to ride the barrels, but it was the only thing he could think of that might help.

"I always ride that way when I'm barrel racing," she told him. "And I also tried everything else I could think of but nothing worked." She got a scoop of oats from the bin to feed her horse. "I don't have any trouble with Patches, but Sawdust is something else."

She paused for an instant and he noted a certain reluctance in her voice. "I hate to admit it, Greg, but I'm beginning to believe that I'll never make a barrel racer of him. He's so afraid of those barrels he won't do what I want him to."

"I could go out tomorrow night and see if I can help you with him," he suggested. "That is, if you want me to."

"I'd sure like your help, if you think it would do any good."

He shrugged expressively. "You know horses

as well as I do. The only advantage is that I've got more strength in my arms. I might be able to hold him in situations where you couldn't."

She leaned against the manger. "I'm ready to try anything."

He could understand exactly how she felt. It reminded him of the time when he trained Patches. He had thought the horse would never reach the place where he would respond the way he should.

Kim must have been thinking about the same thing. "How did you manage training your horse?" she asked.

"It wasn't easy." He reached over and stroked the young gelding's nose. "You want to remember that Patches is six years old now and has been roping and barrel racing since he was three. Sawdust just turned three and was only broke to ride a year ago. It's no wonder that he's green and afraid of the barrels."

Kim's smile brightened. "Do you really think that's the reason?"

"The way I see it, you're going to have to spend a lot of time working with him to get him over his fear of the barrels and that pesky shying."

"Was Patches ever like that?"

"Was he ever! Don't you remember?"

She nodded.

"Every horse is different. Sawdust is afraid of the barrels. You'll have to work with him until he gets over it."

Dismay clouded her eyes. "I guess that ends the barrel racing for me this year. And competing in the Little Mavericks' Rodeo."

"You can ride Patches," Greg told her.

She stared at her brother in surprise. "You can't be serious!"

"Try me." He shut off the lights and together they started for the house.

They went inside, shedding their jackets and hanging them in the back hall before going into the kitchen where their parents and Kevin were sitting.

"I can't do it, Greg," she continued. "Patches is your horse and you're planning on entering the goat tying and breakaway roping. You can't have him all worn out before you start."

"He won't run more than a few seconds in each go-round," Greg reminded her. "Not even enough to get him warmed up."

"But I—I'd ride him a lot more than that. There are three go-rounds in barrel racing."

"One each day," he said. "Besides, the barrel racing is usually after breakaway roping, so I'll get him when he's fresh."

Greg saw that it took a moment or so for Kim to realize that he was serious. He read the doubt in her eyes and saw it give way to concern and then incredulity. "You—you really meant that I—I can actually ride Patches in the Little Mavericks' Rodeo?"

He nodded. "If you want to."

"If I want to! Oh, Greg!" she exclaimed, impulsively taking a step toward him. "That's just about the nicest thing anyone has done for me in a long time. I—I could kiss you!"

He drew away quickly. "Try that and the

deal's off," he muttered.

The following week was warm and sunny. By Tuesday night the last of the snow had melted and by Friday most of the mud puddles had dried or were well along in the process of drying. Frank sought out Hip and Greg that afternoon as soon as classes were out to make sure they were going to visit the Lazy H the following day.

"Now," he said, "you don't have any excuse for not coming out to watch me ride."

Hip's grin was contagious. "Is that why you want us to visit the ranch tomorrow?"

Frank's frown deepened and his gaze swept the slight figure of the young Chicano. "Not exactly." Contempt edged his voice. "Uncle Lee said that I *had* to invite you if I asked Greg to come out. That's why you got the chance to come along."

Greg Powell winced. He knew what Frank meant by his remark and hoped Hip hadn't caught it. But a quick glance at his friend's taut features showed that he had. Hip's cheeks crimsoned and for an instant he looked away.

"*You* didn't want me. Is that it?" he asked evenly.

Frank seemed embarrassed. "I didn't say that I didn't want you."

"He didn't intend it to sound the way it did," Greg put in quickly.

"That's right. I just meant that Uncle Lee said to be sure and invite you if I asked Greg. He didn't want you to be left out."

The Powell boy had the feeling that Frank

wasn't telling the truth, but Hip changed the subject. "So, you want to show us how well you can ride!"

Frank nodded. "Right on!" He paused momentarily. "I'll admit it. I want you stupes to see that I can ride. I want to show you that you're not the only ones who can stick on a horse."

"We'll be there," Greg assured him.

The next morning shortly after eight o'clock, the boys loaded Patches and Hip's horse, Spangler, into the trailer and George Powell drove them out to the Lazy H. Frank had already saddled a fiesty two-year-old that had been broken only a few weeks before. He leaned forward in the saddle and flailed the hard-running horse with a supple willow switch, dashing at full speed to meet the pickup.

As the boys and Mr. Powell watched, Frank whipped the horse past the vehicle and trailer, jerked him across the lane in a tight U-turn and headed back toward the ranch buildings.

"What's he trying to do?" Greg muttered.

His dad shrugged. "He's trying to show us how fast his horse can go, I reckon."

"That's stupid. He can't beat a truck."

Hip turned in the seat and watched as the vehicle pulled past the hard galloping horse and rider. "He sure wasn't lying when he said he could ride," the Mexican boy acknowledged grudgingly. "He's plenty good."

"He can also abuse a horse," Greg reminded him.

"I was thinking the same thing," his dad said.

"If he abused an animal of mine that way, he wouldn't get to ride again, that's for sure."

When Greg opened the pickup door and got out, Frank had stopped his mount not a dozen feet away. His hands were clasped about the saddle horn and he was resting his weight against his arms.

"Well," he said, a tantalizing, superior little smile lighting his usually somber features, "what do you think now? Can I ride or can't I?"

Trembling slightly, Greg went over to the horse and wiped a finger across the corner of the poor animal's mouth where the bit had cut into tender flesh on the turn. "Blood!" he said angrily.

"So—?"

"Your uncle shouldn't allow you to ride again. Nobody has the right to treat animals this way."

Frank was arrogant. "You've got to show an ornery beast like this who's boss," he retorted carelessly. "If he'd behaved himself, I wouldn't have had to handle him rough, would I?"

Greg's gaze met his evenly. "Let's don't do that again. OK?"

At first he was surprised that Frank accepted the reprimand without arguing. Then Greg saw that Mr. Huffman was approaching and he realized why the rancher's nephew had been so meek.

"Come on," Frank said, changing the subject. "I'll help you guys get your horses out of the trailer so we can get started." He swung himself to the ground and tied his horse to the front bumper of the pickup. "Uncle Lee and one of the hands helped me get some calves in the chute."

It was decided that Hipolita would rope first. He checked Spangler's cinch, mounted, and shook out his first loop, swinging the rope back and forth with an easy wrist motion. The second lariat was curled about the saddle horn within easy reach. He rode his roan cow pony into the corral and took his place beside the starting gate.

Greg reached for the swinging frame to release the lever that held it in place. "Tell me when you're ready."

Hipolita tightened his grip on the reins with his left hand and once more shook out the loop. "Go!"

Greg jerked open the gate and, suddenly realizing that he was free, the calf exploded into the arena. Once the wiry, hard-running little animal cleared the barrier, Hip shouted a command to Spangler and dug his heels into the horse's flanks.

It all happened in a sudden blur of speed. In three long, distance-gobbling strides, Spangler put Hip within roping distance of the calf. The stiff loop snaked out, settling inches short of the young steer's head. Hip groaned his disappointment and in one smooth motion dropped the rope to the ground, snatched up the spare and sent the loop sailing in the direction of the calf's head. It, too, fell short.

"Hey, man, that was the pits!" Frank called out. "It won't do you any good to enter the rodeo if you can't do a lot better'n that."

Greg read the disappointment in his pal's eyes. "Don't let it get to you," he said. "You haven't thrown a rope all winter. You'll do OK when you get your hand in."

"I'll have to show you how it's done," Frank boasted. "Watch close and you both can pick up a few pointers."

It was Greg's turn next. Like Hipolita, he hadn't thrown a rope at a moving target since fall and his timing was badly off. He missed his first loop, but fortunately, caught the calf with the second. The instant the rope dropped over the animal's head and tightened, the string tying it to the saddle horn broke, letting the rope fall free.

Then it was Frank's turn. Hip gave Greg a gleeful look. Greg knew Hip was thinking Frank would try to rope from the young horse, but they were mistaken. Frank was too knowledgeable for that. Unhurriedly he took the saddle off the two-year-old and saddled Blaze, a seasoned cow pony, who knew every move to make. Once the saddle was in place he mounted and shook out the first rope.

"Now," he said confidently, "watch how a *pro* does it."

Greg felt like telling him to get with it and do his bragging with his rope, but decided that wouldn't be wise. He would show himself up soon enough. Frank took his place at the gate and signaled for Greg to release the calf.

The moment the calf left the chute, the rider was after him. "You broke the barrier!" Greg shouted to the wind. "No time!"

But Frank wasn't listening. His rope found the calf's head and one front foot a few yards in front of the chutes.

"There!" he exclaimed triumphantly, as he came back to where his companions were waiting. "How was that?"

"OK."

Frank snorted. "OK? Is that all you can say? Neither you nor Hip connected. I guess I've shown you who's the roper of this outfit. And I was fast, too! I wish somebody'd been timing me."

"You broke the barrier," Greg informed him. "In a real rodeo you'd have been disqualified."

Frank shook his head in disgust. "You're somethin' else! Let a guy beat you and the first thing you do is cry, 'foul!' " He turned away. "You make me sick!"

5.

Frank insisted on trying again.

"I'm going to prove to you two that it wasn't a fluke the last time," he boasted.

"We believe you," Hip said.

Frank laughed. "You sure sound like it. But just you wait. I'll show you in the Little Mavericks' Rodeo. I'll walk all over you characters and anybody else who's stupid enough to enter against me."

Greg frowned. He didn't see why Frank had to be so gross. . . . Well, he and Hip'd show him! He didn't care what happened. They both were going to beat that dude from Illinois in the real rodeo. This stuff didn't count. Let him show off now. It was the real thing that people were going to pay attention to.

Greg and Hip soon discovered that Frank's first try had not been an accident. They didn't know where he had learned to handle a rope, but he was good. He nailed his first calf a dozen paces from the chute and the next a couple of steps farther. His rope snapped out like a thing alive, to fall with unerring accuracy over the calf's head. He caught the third calf with the same skill, and when he dismounted and strolled back to his friends he swaggered slightly.

"Your turn now," he murmured. "That'll give you something to shoot at."

"You can say that again," Hipolita told him.

Frank paused and turned, smirking. "I've been trying to tell you I'm good, but you haven't believed me."

Greg looked away deliberately. "I guess I'm ready."

Frank laughed. "Want me to leave?" he asked.

"Leave? Why'd I want that?"

"So you won't be so embarrassed when you mess everything up."

Greg roped his first calf sloppily, but managed to get the loop on him. His second was a bit better. Then Hipolita managed to rope two in succession in what would probably have been acceptable time.

"Not bad," Frank said. "Not bad at all. If it wasn't for me you'd have a fair chance of winning the breakaway roping event."

Greg scowled and busied himself with his saddle so he could pretend not to hear Frank's boasting.

His dad came back to the Lazy H late that afternoon to pick up his son, Hipolita and their horses.

"Coming out again next Saturday?" Frank asked when they had the animals loaded in the trailer.

Greg shrugged. "That depends."

"I can get Uncle Lee to come after you with his horse trailer," Frank said. His expression changed. "I can get him to do anything I want him to."

"I wouldn't bet on that if I were you."

Bernard Palmer

"It's the truth. I could do the same thing when
I lived back in Moline. If I wanted anything all I
had to do was to beg Dad until I got it." He
chuckled quietly.

"Except when he got mad at me. Then, wow! I
was sure he was goin' to cane me!"

"That kind of stuff wouldn't do me any good,"
Greg said. "If I tried anything like that, Dad'd
give me a lickin' 'til I couldn't sit down for a
week."

Frank was still laughing. "That happened to
me one time," he said. "A friend of mine and I
got into Dad's bar when he was away and got a
bottle of his best wine. We drank it all and got a
little high."

"That wasn't very smart, if you ask me,"
Hipolita said.

"I didn't ask you." He acted as though he
expected his companions to either be shocked or
to ask him about it and was disappointed when
they did neither.

"It was sure fun," he added defensively.

Hipolita stared at him. "My dad used to drink
a lot before he was a Christian," he said. "I
know all about how much *fun* it is. I know how
much fun it was for him to be sick from drinking
and not able to work, and I know how much fun
it was for the rest of us when he lost his job
because of his drinking and we hardly had
anything in the house to eat."

"I'll have to show you how much fun it is,"
Frank repeated.

Before they could reply Mr. Powell and
Frank's uncle appeared. Mr. Huffman invited

them to come back any time to practice for the upcoming rodeo. They thanked him and got into the pickup.

No one said much until they reached the city limits of Concord and Greg's dad slowed to the city speed limit. "You guys have no idea how grateful Mr. Huffman is to you for befriending his nephew. He says he has got to do everything he can to help Frank adjust to his parents' divorce."

"Frank sure doesn't act as though it bothers him that much," Hipolita put in.

Mr. Powell slowed and turned into the drive at their house. "Lee wondered if you boys would ask Frank to go to Sunday school and church with us."

Greg's eyelids flew open and he stared unblinkingly at his dad. "He wasn't serious about that, was he?"

"Serious enough to volunteer to bring him into town every Sunday so he can go with us." They got out of the half-ton truck and went around to the rear of the trailer to unload the horses.

"He made me very proud of you boys and Kim. He said he has been watching you when you've been out at the ranch and he likes what he sees. He figures maybe Sunday school and church would have a good effect on his nephew."

"It might if we could get him there," Greg murmured. "I've got a hunch we'd have to rope him and tie him with a piggin' string to get him to Sunday school."

George Powell shook his head. "Maybe.

Bernard Palmer

Maybe not. We'll never know until we try, will we?"

The next week saw spring come to the high plains of eastern Colorado. Buffalo grass began to shed its brown winter coat, replacing it with a tinge of faded green, and prairie flowers burst into bloom. The southern breezes were warm and kindly and the sun's soft rays brushed the hills with a gentle kiss.

Kim didn't say much about the rodeo around home. When she did Kevin teased her about thinking she had a chance in the barrel race. So she kept silent, even when Greg and Hipolita jabbered about the Little Mavericks' Rodeo—which seemed to be all the time they were together. Yet, she thought about it as much as they did. Especially now that Greg had said she could ride Patches. He could make the difference between sure defeat and a chance at winning.

Kim wouldn't be entering the roping or goat tying events. They had to be left to girls who were raised on a ranch where they could practice long hours every day. But she said, as far as she was concerned, barrel racing was just as important. More so, maybe. It seemed to her that the crowd was always excited about the race and saved their loudest cheers for the girls who did well in the mad scramble around the barrels. Always before she had watched longingly while her friends competed. Now she was excited about being out there herself.

When she was in bed at night she would

imagine the crowd in the bleachers at the Lazy
H. She told Greg of a dream she had one night.
The breakaway calf roping and calf riding had
just ended and it was time for the cloverleaf
barrel race. She was astride Patches, nervously
getting him into position.

"Go!" she cried when she felt that everything
was right. She leaned forward and dug her heels
into his flanks. He exploded across the line on a
dead run, pounding toward the first barrel. He
was so experienced she had only to lay the rein
across his neck to turn him in a tight arc about
the barrel. He cut so close to it fear leaped within
her that the rush of air or the slight touch of his
hip would send the barrel rolling, but it didn't
move. The same was true of the second barrel.
On her way around the third a great exultation
surged within her. She was making the best
run she had ever made. She was going to win!
She knew it!

Then, the last contestant had ridden and the
race was over. She saw herself triumphantly
walking Patches back to the judges where they
announced that she had just turned in a Little
Mavericks' record for the barrel race and
presented her with the trophy.

That race had only been a dream, to be sure,
but it could happen. And if she worked hard
enough, it was going to happen! That she
promised herself.

Kim took advantage of the new season by
riding Greg's horse out to the fairgrounds every
afternoon for a long workout with the barrels.
Kevin even talked her into letting him ride

Sawdust on occasion—so he could be there to help her, he said. He set up the barrels when she knocked them over and used the stopwatch to time her on the course. She was doing well enough that even her younger brother was impressed, though he tried hard to keep her from knowing it.

"How'd I do on that last run?" she wanted to know.

He glanced at the watch. "It was heavy, Kim! Real heavy!"

Disgust welled within her. She didn't know why younger brothers had to be so gross. "What did I do?" she demanded. "What was my time?"

He studied the watch again. "Let's see. It was under two minutes."

"Kevin!"

"Well, it was! You were even under one minute."

"I have to know!" she exploded.

"Let me think. Two and two is four, times six. That makes—"

"You won't get to come out here on Sawdust if you don't shape up," she warned darkly. "I'll *never* let you ride him again."

"Don't get so uptight about it," he countered. "Your time was 25.01 seconds."

Kim gasped.

"Don't get yourself all hoked up over a little thing like that," Kevin reminded her. "Patches did all the work. You just went along for the ride."

She stuck her tongue out at him. "Brothers!" she exclaimed.

While Kevin helped Kim with her barrel racing, Greg and Hip were striving to make friends with Frank. And it wasn't all that easy. One day at school he would be warm and friendly. The next he was short-tempered, acting as though he scarcely knew them.

"Why don't you invite him home with you for supper, Hipolita?" Mrs. Rodriguez asked her son as he and Greg sat at the kitchen table having cookies and milk.

Hip's cheeks colored slightly and he acted as though he hadn't heard her.

"Why don't you?" she repeated.

"It won't do any good," he said. "He won't come."

She stopped what she was doing and came over to the table. "What makes you so sure of that?"

"Because I know him!" he retorted angrily. "That's why!" He pulled in a deep breath. "He doesn't like *our* kind of people."

She hesitated. "You mean he wouldn't come because we're Mexican Americans?"

"That's not what *he* calls us! He calls us Chicanos and makes it sound like a swear word!"

Mrs. Rodriguez turned to Greg. "Do you think Frank would come over here if he was invited?"

He paused momentarily. "I don't know for sure. . . . He says that he likes Hip. . . ."

"He sure doesn't act like it!" the young Chicano blurted.

"Half the time he doesn't act as though he likes me or anybody else, either," Greg

Bernard Palmer

reminded him. "You know how he is."

Hipolita still was not convinced. "Go ahead and invite him, Mom," he said. "You'll see."

Greg wished that he and Hipolita could forget all about Frank Ellis and making friends with him, but they couldn't. They had promised to try to persuade him to go to Sunday school and church. Thursday came and went and they still had not even talked to him.

Greg didn't know whether Hip had talked his mother out of inviting Frank over for supper or if she had changed her mind on her own, but he heard nothing more about it the rest of the week. He had hoped maybe she would invite Frank to eat with them so she or her husband could ask him about going to Sunday school and church.

When it looked as though that invitation wasn't going to be coming from the Rodriguez family, he tried to talk his mother into having the Ellis boy over. Then his dad could do the asking about his coming to Sunday school and church, but that didn't work, either. Mrs. Powell already had one set of guests coming that weekend and she couldn't work in any more.

"Besides," she said pointedly, "this is something you promised to do. It's your problem."

He felt his cheeks blanch. He didn't know how mothers could sense what a guy was planning without being told. Sometimes it gave him the creeps the way she could look into his mind. But what she had said was true enough. It was the responsibility of himself and Hipolita. There was no way of squirming out of it.

"It would be different," he told his pal as they left the Rodriguez home for school Friday morning, "if we had a chance of getting him to go with us. But I don't think any of the talking that we or anybody else can do is going to help. That character's not goin' to do anything he doesn't want to do."

Hipolita picked up a large pebble on the grass beside the walk, weighed it momentarily in his hand and chucked it out into the street. It bounced to the opposite side and came to rest a few inches from the curb. "But that's not the point. We've got to try—even if he does make fun of us. We told your dad we would."

"Yeah," Greg echoed. "It's tough, but we've got to try." Frank would probably laugh in their faces and make a big joke of it around school, but they had to make an effort to get him to go with them.

Greg drew in a long, deep breath and expelled the air in a thin stream. He really wanted to see Frank start going to Sunday school and church. It was obvious that he knew nothing about Jesus Christ, let alone putting his trust in Him for salvation. If Greg was honest with himself, however, he had to admit that he didn't like Frank all that much. He really wasn't the sort of guy he wanted to make friends with.

When they reached the school building that morning Frank was entering just ahead of them. Greg couldn't help thinking that he acted as though he owned the place.

Frank stopped and turned slowly, a thin, sneering smile forming on his lips. "Here come the great All-American cowboys."

"You said it," Hipolita answered, as though the remark had been meant as a compliment.

Frank moved closer. "You think you're goin' to have a chance of winning something at the rodeo, but let me clue you, you're wastin' your time. You've got *me* to compete against."

"Don't tell us that," Greg replied. "Let us have our dreams. OK?"

"I tried out a new roping horse last night," Frank confided. Strangely, the braggadocio disappeared and he was almost congenial. "Uncle Lee's personal roping horse. And is he good!"

The more he talked, the louder his voice crescendoed until it could be heard half the distance of the long, tunnel-like corridor. "I did so great last night I even surprised myself!"

Greg winced as Frank started down the hall with him and Hipolita. "I'd like to tell you my times but Uncle Lee made me promise not to. He was afraid too many of the guys would decide not to enter in my events if they knew how good I was."

Greg tried to ignore the now commonplace boasting. He had something else on his mind. Something he had to do that morning. He struggled for words and it was not until they were in the hall outside their home room that he finally found the courage to ask the other boy to go to Sunday school and church.

Frank's eyelids drooped suspiciously. "Do you really want me there," he demanded, his tone surly, "or are you asking because you have to?"

"What do you mean by that?"

"Uncle Lee told me Saturday that you were going to talk to me about it this week, but you didn't say anything until right now." His voice raised accusingly. "How come?"

"I guess we were afraid you would turn us down," Hipolita replied frankly. "And we were trying to get up courage to talk to you about it."

Frank Ellis turned the statement over in his mind. "You're putting me on."

"I'm givin' it to you straight. Isn't that right, Greg?"

The taller boy nodded his affirmation.

There was a long, embarrassed silence. "I don't know whether to believe you or not, but I do know this. I'm goin' to fool you both!"

"Just how do you figure on doing that?" Greg asked.

"I've decided to go with you—just once—to see what it's like."

"Hey, that's great!" Hipolita exclaimed.

"Besides," Frank continued, grinning, "Uncle Lee promised me a new saddle if I'd go with you every Sunday for six months."

Greg felt as though someone had thrown a bucket of cold water on him. He shivered involuntarily.

6.

Bernard Palmer

In spite of Frank's assurance that he would be in for church services that Sunday morning Greg and Hipolita were the only ones who expected him. They were the only ones who knew about the saddle. Greg thought about it every time the subject came up at home, but he didn't feel free to mention it—even to his parents.

"We aren't going to have to wait for Frank this morning, are we, Dad?" Kevin asked as the Powells sat around the breakfast table.

Mr. Powell shook his head. "Lee said he could have him here by 9:30. He'll be here on time if he's coming."

They had finished eating and were almost ready to leave for Sunday school when they heard a pickup pull into the driveway and stop. Kevin jumped to his feet and looked out.

"There he is!" he exclaimed. "And right on the stick—9:30."

Greg reached the porch in time to see Mr. Huffman back into the street and drive away in the direction of the Concord business district.

Frank Ellis strutted up the steps. "I'll bet you thought I wasn't going to show," he said, striding past Greg into the living room.

"I figured you'd be here."

"You could bet on it. I'm not goin' to miss out on that new saddle. Went in and picked one out

62

yesterday. You ought to see it! Covered with hand tooling. You'll never have a saddle like it as long as you live."

Kevin and Kim came into the living room just then and Frank changed the subject abruptly, asking what time Sunday school got out and if they had to stay for church.

"We always do," they told him.

He sighed his annoyance. "I guess that's about what I expected of you." He turned back to the front door as the family started to leave for Sunday school.

Hipolita and his folks had arrived at church a few minutes earlier and he was waiting for Greg and Frank on the front steps of the church building. They went into their class together.

"Nobody had better call on me to say anything," the visitor muttered uneasily. "If they do, I'm splittin'. Saddle or no saddle."

"Mr. Edwards will probably ask you to introduce yourself," Hip told him. "It's your first time in class and he usually does that with newcomers."

"That's not what I mean."

Greg didn't know whether Frank had ever been in Sunday school before, but he seemed to enjoy it in spite of the fact that he did not take part in the discussion.

When the class was over he turned to his companions, concern marking his face. "Is that true?" he asked seriously.

Greg didn't know what he was talking about and said so.

"What Mr. Edwards told us about God

answering prayer."

"Sure, it's true."

But Frank was still not satisfied. "Have you ever had any prayers answered?"

"Lots of times."

Frank's features reflected his disbelief. "You aren't stringin' me, are you?"

"Greg's right on," Hipolita put in. "Practically every week God answers one of my prayers about something."

They left the classroom and started for the stairs to the main floor. A strange wistfulness stole across the newcomer's face. "Do you mean to tell me that He'll do anything we ask Him to?"

Greg thought for a moment or more before shaking his head. "Well, it's not quite as simple as that," he began. "God always hears our prayers if we're children of His—if we've confessed our sin and put our trust in Him. But He doesn't always give us everything we ask for. What we pray for might not be good for us."

He was about to say more but the other boy broke in quickly.

"Oh, this would. It would be the best thing that could ever happen to me."

Greg and Hipolita eyed him curiously. The sudden fervor in his voice surprised them. He noticed that they were studying him and his face darkened with embarrassment. It was almost as though they had caught him doing something he shouldn't, and guilt flushed his cheeks.

All through the service he sat as one in a

trance. When the rest of the congregation stood to sing he stood with them, and when they sat down he did the same. But his eyes were glazed and he stared straight ahead, as though his mind was transported a thousand miles to the east. He scarcely moved throughout the entire message and when it was over his preoccupation continued. He was extraordinarily quiet as he rode home with the Powells and waited on the front porch for his uncle.

"Are you positive about that prayer bit?" he asked Greg again.

"Sure. Why?"

Frank shifted from one foot to the other uneasily. "I don't know. It just seems sort of funny to me, that's all." His uncle's pickup turned the corner a block away and headed toward the Powell house. He saw it and grinned, suddenly arrogant again. "You'd never catch me praying, that's for sure. I can't swallow that stuff."

At school the next day he was no more friendly than before. He pranced over to where Greg and Hipolita were sitting, insolence in every move. He slammed his tray on the table across from them, jerked out a chair and sat down.

"The great ropers!" he exclaimed, his high pitched voice carrying to the farthest corner of the room.

Greg shrugged with feigned indifference. There was no use in having trouble with Frank if he could avoid it. He was going to have to put up with him for a while longer if he and Hip were going to use the Lazy H to work out for the Little Mavericks' Rodeo.

"A week from next Saturday I figure on showing you two up—but good! Uncle Lee's havin' a little rodeo—sort of a tuneup for the big one. So I've got a chance to show you bums how good I am."

"Sounds great," Hip exclaimed. "Eh, Greg?"

"It sure does." They had been practicing roping calves at the Lazy H and felt that they were making progress, but being in actual competition was something else. It would show them if they were actually getting any better.

"You won't be so thrilled when I get through with you," Frank continued. "And that's a promise."

By this time he realized that he had an audience and would have said more but Mark Thieben and Don Gressert came over and asked about the rodeo. They wanted to enter too.

Frank frowned and for the first time uncertainty crept into his voice. "I'm not sure about that," he said. "Uncle Lee didn't say anything about inviting outsiders for this one."

Mark eyed Greg and Hip quizzically. "What about *them?*" he demanded.

Frank seemed embarrassed. "According to Uncle Lee," he said defensively, "they're special."

"Yeah. Special!" Don marked the air with his finger, tracing a big square.

"I know it's gross," Frank continued, "but I can't help it."

"Maybe not, but you c'n talk to him for us,

can't you?"

"Yeah, you can talk to your uncle," Don said, glaring pointedly at Greg and Hipolita. "Tell him that we'll be in Sunday school every week, too."

Their laughter rang out in the room.

Greg hadn't finished eating but he pushed his plate aside. "C'mon, Hip. Let's get out of here."

The young Chicano followed suit. Once they were outside Hip turned to Greg. "Those guys are bad medicine."

"You can say that again. I hope Frank doesn't start running around with them."

The next day or so they saw little of the rancher's nephew outside the classroom. He spoke to them when he saw them, but that was all. Greg had the feeling that Frank was avoiding them. He didn't know why but he suspected that it had something to do with Don and Mark. Then, on Thursday morning he sought out Greg uneasily. He had a problem, he said, and didn't know what to do about it.

"Uncle Lee and Aunt Florence are going to leave for Denver tomorrow night," he confided, "and be gone for the weekend. I won't have anyone to stay with, so it looks as though I'll have to go along." He paused and leaned forward slightly. "That means I'd miss Sunday school and church."

"That's too bad." Greg didn't know why he said that. He wasn't sure he meant it, but he felt that he had to say something and the words slipped out.

"Yeah . . . and I sure hate it."

67

Bernard Palmer

"What's the matter? Are you afraid you won't earn your new saddle?" Greg blurted. He hadn't intended to say that either.

Frank shook his head. "I didn't even think about that," he continued. "If Uncle Lee took me out of town, he wouldn't hold that against me—missing Sunday school, I mean." He laid a hand on Greg's arm. "I *really* want to go."

"I'll talk to Mom if you want me to," Greg said, "and see if you can stay with us."

Frank brightened. "You're a pal!"

Greg couldn't quite understand his friend's excitement at getting to go to Sunday school the following weekend. As far as he was concerned it was completely out of character.

"We've all been prayin' for Frank," Kevin said that night when the subject came up during family devotions. "Maybe God is beginning to work."

Greg wanted to believe that but he had the uneasy feeling that it was something else. He wasn't sure just what.

Mrs. Huffman brought her nephew's suitcase to the Powell house the following afternoon and Frank went home with Greg from school.

"I wish we could get out to the Lazy H alone tomorrow," Frank said. "We'd really have ourselves a blast."

Greg eyed him questioningly.

"I know where Uncle Lee keeps the key to the cabinet his booze is in." He lowered his voice although there was no one else within half a block. "Man, he has got it *all!* Beer—wine—vodka—whiskey—a regular cocktail lounge.

68

And for free!"

The Powell boy frowned. He knew there were guys out at school who dipped into their dad's liquor. They boasted about it afterward. But they all knew where he stood. This was the first time he'd ever been offered anything.

"You've got to be kiddin'!"

Frank grinned. "That's what it's for, ain't it?"

"Not in *my* book!"

Frank eyed him impishly.

Sunday morning Frank was ready to go to services before anyone else in the family. And all during Sunday school and church he listened intently.

"Well," Greg said when it was over and they were on their way outside again, "what did you think of it this morning?"

"It was all right, I guess." Disappointment edged his voice.

"Didn't you like it?"

Frank shrugged. "I thought they'd spend more time praying and stuff, like they did last week in Sunday school."

"The teacher does that once a month."

The rancher's nephew stared at him. "Why?" he asked. "Aren't people supposed to pray more than once a month?"

"Sure. We're supposed to pray all the time."

"Then why does the teacher do it only once a month in class? I don't get it."

"He has got a lot of things about being a Christian to teach us," Greg explained. "He can't spend all the time on one thing."

On the steps just outside the church door

Frank paused and turned to his companion. "Give it to me straight," he exclaimed suddenly. "Does it *really* do any good to pray?"

The other boy's eyelids narrowed. This wasn't the first time Frank had talked to him about that. It seemed as though he had something on his mind—something he didn't want anyone else to know about.

"Does it?" he repeated.

"Sure it does."

"I mean, has God ever answered any big prayers for you? I mean *really* big?"

"Sure he has!"

"Like what?"

Greg had to think about that. There were lots of times when God had answered prayers that seemed big to him, but he didn't know whether Frank would feel that way about them.

"There was the time Patches had distemper and the vet didn't know whether or not he would live. We all prayed and he got well, almost right away."

"Yeah?" The question in Frank's voice urged him on.

"And there was the time when Dad lost his job and couldn't find anything to do. The paper he worked for was sold and the new owner brought in his own reporters and photographers. We prayed about it and three days later he had a call from the paper here."

The other boy waited. "Is that all?"

"That's all I can think of right now.... Why?"

The color crept into Frank's cheeks and spread from his ears across the bridge of his nose. "I was just wonderin'."

They continued down the church steps and got into the car together.

"I was just wonderin' if it does any good to ask God for things you want awful bad." For an instant his lips quivered and Greg expected tears to come to his eyes.

"Of course you've got to meet God's conditions before He'll answer your prayers," Greg said.

Frank's lips tightened. "You mean there's a catch to it?"

"You might say that. He just doesn't promise to answer the prayers of those who haven't confessed their sin and put their trust in Jesus to save them."

Frank paused for a time. "I don't get it."

Greg was trying to find words to frame a reply when Kevin and Kimberly came bursting out to the car, arguing about who would sit in the front seat. That cut off any serious conversation.

He hoped he would have another chance to talk to Frank about prayer and receiving Christ as his Saviour, but he didn't that day. They were just finishing dinner when Mr. and Mrs. Huffman came back from Denver and picked him up.

Greg thought he saw a change in Frank at school during the next few days. He seemed happier than before and less cynical and arrogant. He was doing better in his studies, too; so much better their English teacher remarked about it. And Kim, who hadn't liked Frank very well for the way he acted, saw the change in him too.

"Do you suppose it's because he has started going to Sunday school and church with us?" she asked at family devotions one evening in the middle of the week.

"Sure," Kevin said quickly. "What else?"

Greg, however, was not so sure. "When I talked to him Sunday he didn't have the foggiest notion of what it means to be a Christian. All he wanted to talk about was prayer."

Mr. Powell picked up the Bible. "I saw Lee this morning," he said. "He was telling me that Frank got a letter from his mother. His parents are going to a marriage counselor and are thinking about going back together."

"Hey!" Greg exclaimed. "That's great!"

"Lee said that after Frank read the letter he told his Aunt Florence that he has been praying that would happen ever since he started going to Sunday school. He's sure that his prayers are causing the change."

Tears came to Kim's eyes.

Greg was as happy about the new development in Frank's life as the rest of the family, but he couldn't quite square it with what he had been taught about prayer. His folks and the pastor and his Sunday school teacher had always told him that God did not promise to answer the prayers of unbelievers, and they had quoted Bible verses to prove it. If that was true, how could Frank have his prayers answered? Greg couldn't figure it out.

7.

It seemed to Greg that most of the kids in their class had noted the sudden change in Frank and treated him better for it—especially the girls. He still teased them more than he should have probably, but he was more of a gentleman about it. The sneer wasn't as apparent on his mouth and he didn't try to give a dirty twist to everything that was said. At times he was so different that Greg wondered whether Frank might have received Christ as his Saviour and just said nothing about it.

He made up his mind that he was going to ask him, but every time he was with Frank, Mark Thieben or Don Gressert joined them. They hurried over with seeming jealousy, anxious to break into the conversation. Greg had the opinion that they were determined to monopolize Frank.

"I've been wanting to talk to him alone," Greg confided to Hipolita, "but those guys are always hanging around. They act as though they're afraid to leave him alone with us, even for a minute."

"I think it's the rodeo. They sure want to take part."

Greg's eyes slitted. He didn't care whether or not Mark and Don got to compete in the rodeo. He wasn't even concerned with the fact that they might beat him, although that was what they claimed. He just didn't like the idea of Frank being with guys like that. They were always in some kind of trouble. They had broken into one of the classrooms and had stolen the history test papers earlier in the year. And everyone said they were the ones who had robbed the pop machine in the lunchroom over the Christmas holidays, but the authorities had not been able to prove it.

Greg was so concerned about the matter that he talked with his dad about it. Mr. Powell told him he was afraid there was nothing an outsider could do. "Frank's uncle might be able to break it up, but even that would be hard. How could he keep them apart when they're at school?"

"I can't help it," Greg said. "I've got to do something."

At first he thought he would try in spite of his dad's pessimism. The more he thought about it, however, the more reluctant he became. If Frank got mad at him, Greg could lose any chance he might have of helping him. So, instead of trying to convince the rancher's nephew to quit running around with Mark and Don, he decided to pray more consistently than ever about it. He enlisted Kimberly and Kevin to pray with him, also.

Greg was hopeful that the other two boys would not be out at the Lazy H for the impromptu rodeo, but in that he was disappointed. Mr. Powell took Greg, Kim and Hipolita out to the ranch about 9:30 that Saturday, and when they got there Mark and Don were already in the

Bernard Palmer

arena warming up their mounts and loosening
their roping arms before the rodeo started.
Frank was just inside the fence, watching.

"Hey!" Mark shouted as Greg and Hip rode
up. "Look who's here!"

"Ready to get beat?" Don demanded. There
was an unnatural flush in their cheeks and their
voices were loud and boisterous.

"They're goin' to get beat, all right!" Frank
shouted, laughing loudly. "But you're not goin'
to do it! *I* am!"

Don whirled his horse around and rode over to
where Frank leaned against the wooden rails.
Cupping his hands over the saddle horn, he
leaned forward. "I'll lay you ten to five that you
don't even come close to winning."

Mark rode up just in time to overhear the
wager.

"So'll I," he slurred. "How about that?"

Lee Huffman frowned his disapproval, but
said nothing.

Frank laughed his scorn and turned away.

A few minutes later the last of the contestants
and the sparse crowd of spectators had
gathered. The events began. There were timers
and judges and hazers and pickup men like they
would have in the Little Mavericks' Rodeo, but this
one was much more casual and relaxed. There
were frequent delays and much good natured
laughter and bantering.

They had the saddle bronc riding first, then
the team roping before knocking off for the
barbeque Florence Huffman and a couple of
her friends had prepared. Following that, there

was a time for visiting before continuing the rodeo.

They had just finished eating when Lee sought out George Powell and invited him up to the house with a few friends for a quick drink.

"No thank you," Greg's dad said, smiling.

"That's right, you don't drink." The rancher's grin flashed. "I hadn't forgotten. Just wanted to check to be sure you hadn't changed your mind."

"Nope, I'm just as dry as ever."

As the rodeo was about to resume, the announcer called for the bareback riders to gather at the chutes. Everyone began to drift toward the arena.

Kim hurried to catch up with her older brother. "When's the barrel racing?" she asked.

There was no printed program and everything was so haphazard that day no one seemed to know. He shrugged. "You'll have to wait until they announce it."

"Let's go over and ask Frank. He ought to know."

However, he didn't seem to have any more information than they did, and he acted as though he didn't care when each event took place.

"Just don't try to make your barrel run when they're turnin' loose the calves," he told her, laughing boisterously. "That'll get your horse all mixed up."

What he said hadn't seemed so funny to Greg and Kim, but Frank laughed as though it was the best joke he had ever heard.

"What's the matter with you?" Greg asked. He hadn't planned to say that; the question just popped out.

Frank's smile faded. "What do you mean— what's the matter with me?" he echoed. "What makes you think there's anything the matter with me, stupid?"

"No reason. Forget it."

The other boy grabbed Greg by the arm. "No, we won't forget it! What makes you say there's something wrong with me?"

"No reason at all. Just cool it. Put it on ice."

Frank was only partly satisfied. "I don't like havin' anyone make cracks about me. Understand?"

Greg turned away from him deliberately.

The breakaway calf roping was announced just then and Mark was the first roper. He and Don were troublemakers—there was no mistaking that—but they could ride and rope with the best. Greg turned in the best time he had ever had but they both beat him handily.

Frank was off to a good start after his calf. The instant it was released he was on its tail. He would have had the best time for the first go-round, but the wiry little animal kicked free of the first loop. The boy was so angry at that, he had trouble shaking out his second rope and the calf got so far ahead of him it was useless even for him to try. He reined in his cow pony and turned back, his cheeks flushed with embarrassed anger.

Kim fared better in her event than her brother did in his. She finished second with a ride that brought a brief cheer from the crowd. Hip's time was a fraction slower than Greg's, due in part to the fact that his horse hesitated briefly at the start. Still, he made a respectable showing. Both boys did, considering the fact that they hadn't had much time to practice.

"By the time the Little Mavericks' Rodeo comes around we'll be ready," Hip promised confidently. Greg agreed.

Everything considered, it had been a good day for Hipolita and the Powell duo. They had enjoyed every minute of it and were confidently looking forward to the time when they would be able to compete again. Exuberantly they loaded their horses into the trailer and returned to Concord.

Greg hadn't had a chance to say anything to Frank about services the following morning, so he wasn't sure whether or not the rancher's nephew would be there. But he was. At 9:30 Mr. Huffman pulled into the yard in his pickup and let the boy out.

Greg half expected Frank to be arrogant and noisy, but he was just the opposite—far different than he had been the day before. There was a certain excitement in his manner, in spite of the fact that he was quiet and subdued.

Instead of accepting the invitation to come into the Powell house to wait for the family to get their coats on, he asked Greg to come out. The Powell boy did so, curiously.

"You and I were talking about prayer a week or so ago?" Frank began.

Greg nodded.

"Well, it works!"

"Don't tell me that your folks are going back together!" Greg exclaimed.

"They haven't said so for sure," Frank continued, his voice crescendoing, "but I know they are! And it's because I prayed!"

"That's great!"

"You bet it is! I don't mind tellin' you! For me, it's the neatest thing in the whole world!"

The next day at school Greg looked for Frank before classes took up, but the rancher's nephew wasn't around. Greg thought probably something had happened at the ranch to cause him to be late, but he didn't show up all morning. He wasn't in the lunchroom at noon and was absent from his afternoon classes, too.

Kim and Greg talked about it on the way home from school, deciding that he must have been sick. Greg went directly to the living room and dialed the ranch's number. When he hung up moments later, his face was white and drawn.

"What's the matter?" Kim asked.

He paused, unable to form the words immediately. "Mrs. Huffman said that her husband took Frank to town this morning," he said at last. "He let him out in front of the school in plenty of time for his first class."

"But that can't be," Kim protested. "He wasn't there."

"He must have ditched."

"But why would he do a dumb thing like that?" Kim wanted to know.

"Mrs. Huffman said she could understand

why he may have done it. They phoned his mother in Moline last night. She said that everything was off as far as his folks getting back together is concerned. His dad refused to see the marriage counselor after the first visit, so they won't be getting back together again— like Frank was sure they would."

8.

Christine Powell came into the room in time to hear what had happened. "The poor, confused boy!" she exclaimed. "Where is he now?"

"Mrs. Huffman didn't know. She said his uncle went to school after him as usual," Greg said, "and they haven't come back yet."

Mrs. Powell went to the window and looked out, as though she expected to see Frank come hurrying up the walk.

"That's terrible," she murmured. "There's no telling what he might do." She breathed deeply. "Divorce is so hard on the children, especially a boy as sensitive as Frank."

Greg didn't see that Frank was all that sensitive. As far as he could tell, the rancher's nephew was about as insensitive as anyone he knew. But he didn't say anything.

At six o'clock, Mrs. Powell phoned the ranch again and learned that Mr. Huffman and Frank had just returned. He had picked the boy up in front of the school building the same as always. He hadn't even known that Frank hadn't been in school until they got home.

The next morning at school Greg saw Frank, but Frank would scarcely speak to him.

"How're things going?" Greg asked.

"Great!" the other boy exploded. "Just great! Thanks to you!"

"Me? What'd I do?"

"If you don't know, I'm not goin' to tell you!" he snarled.

"What's this all about?"

"You know!"

"If I knew I wouldn't be asking you."

"Your mom called the ranch yesterday afternoon and told Aunt Florence that I wasn't in school. That's what this is all about! She got me in plenty of trouble."

"Mom wasn't the first one to phone your aunt. I was."

Frank's eyes blazed. "That's even worse!"

"I was worried about you. I thought you were sick!"

"Well I wasn't, and you got me in a real mess." His voice trembled angrily. "I hope you're satisfied!"

Greg saw Frank again that morning between classes but when their eyes met, there was no sign of recognition in Frank's stare.

It was the same at noon on the way to the lunchroom. Frank, Don and Mark rushed by, talking boisterously. A minute or two later they chose a table not far from where Greg and Hip were sitting.

"Watch 'em now!" Frank exclaimed, snickering his disdain. "They'll be prayin' in a minute."

Crimson crept into Greg's cheeks and he looked away quickly, hoping no one else had heard what Frank said.

That afternoon in history class, Frank Ellis caused a disturbance and was sent to the principal's office. Don and Mark both snickered as he got to his feet and swaggered out into the hall. Greg was afraid he might go outside the school grounds instead of where he was supposed to go and get himself in even more trouble, but he didn't. He came back after the class was over and went to the library.

"I wish we were out at the ranch right now," he said to Mark and Don, loudly enough for Greg and Hipolita to hear. "After that hassle I could do with a cold beer."

"Me too," Don murmured.

Greg was sure that he had seen the last of Frank at Sunday services in spite of the fact that the entire Powell family had been praying about it. Frank had seemed so indifferent and calloused the last few days that Greg had the impression that he didn't care about anything—especially anything that had to do with Jesus Christ. Nevertheless, when 9:30 rolled around on Sunday morning the Lazy H pickup pulled into the yard and stopped to let the boy out.

"Hey, Greg!" Kevin exclaimed, "Frank's here! He came after all!"

Frank came up the steps and punched the door bell. Greg went to let him in.

"All set to listen to those hypocrites at church?" the rancher's nephew demanded.

Greg's eyelids narrowed. "If you feel that way," he said quietly, "why did you come?"

"Have you forgotten about the saddle I'm supposed to get for bein' a good little boy and attending Sunday school and church every week?"

Greg admitted that he had.

"Well I haven't or I wouldn't be here." He breathed deeply. "It's all a big farce, you know."

"What makes you say that?" Greg demanded.

"Because it is," Frank stepped inside, his gaze fixed on Greg's for some sign of shock. "I took in everything you and that Sunday school teacher said about prayer." He lowered his voice. "I bought it all. The whole ball of wax! I even made a fool of myself by tellin' Don and Mark that I'd been prayin' and I knew God was going to fix things so my folks'd call off that stupid divorce and let me go back to live with them."

The hurt was deep in his eyes. "And look what happened! Things are worse than ever between Mom and Dad and I'll prob'ly *never* get to go back to Moline to live with them!"

Greg didn't know what to say about that. He knew that Frank hadn't met God's conditions for answering prayer. He hadn't confessed his sin and put his trust in Christ for salvation. But even if he did receive Christ, it didn't mean that God would answer all of his prayers the way he wanted them answered. There are times when God says no to us—even about things we think are the most important, Greg knew.

He tried to explain that to his friend but Frank was scarcely listening. His lower lip quivered and for an instant he acted as though he was about to start crying.

"Big deal!" he muttered darkly. "As far as I'm concerned, I've had it with religion—up to here!" He made a cutting motion across his throat with his hand. "The only reason I'm goin' any more is to get that saddle! And when I've earned it, I'll be long gone! You won't see me around this dump any more."

Greg wanted to say more to him, but could think of nothing more to say.

That morning Frank made it apparent to everyone that he had little respect for the church and no interest whatever in what was going on. He slouched into the Sunday school room, dropped to a chair in the corner and leaned back against the wall, deliberately ignoring everyone else. In church he scooted down in the pew, braced his knees against the back of the seat ahead and closed his eyes, feigning sleep. He seemed to delight in the fact that people around him were looking his direction, disapproval in their eyes.

"Dad," Greg said when the family was alone at the dinner table that noon, "it doesn't do any good to try and work with Frank anymore. I can tell you right now that he's not going to receive Christ."

"Oh, don't say that," his mother broke in quickly. "We should never give up on anyone."

"That's easy enough to say," Greg countered, "but there's no use fooling ourselves about Frank."

He saw by his mother's frown that she didn't approve of what he had said. She believed that a guy shouldn't give up on anyone. The trouble was that she didn't really know Frank. If she did, she'd realize how useless it was to keep on working with him.

Nevertheless, Greg felt sorry for the rancher's nephew. The next few days probably were more difficult for Frank than any he had put in since moving out to the Lazy H. He made more trouble in class than ever. When the teacher was called out of the room, even for a moment or two, Frank was sure to have things in an uproar when she returned. And his grades were terrible. He flunked an easy English quiz that he should have made a perfect score on, and failed a tougher test in math which was his favorite subject.

He pulled the hair of the girl who sat in front of him, jerking it so hard she cried, then laughed at her when he saw the tears. He threw spit balls at Don and Mark and turned the teacher's wastebasket upside down on the desk of a new girl who was so shy most of the kids hadn't yet been able to get acquainted with her. She cried in embarrassment and frustration, to Frank's glee.

"Hey, Mark!" he exclaimed loudly. "A crybaby! Isn't it too bad she spilled all her papers? Miss Donnelson isn't going to like that."

The new girl wiped at her eyes, her cheeks scarlet.

Frank leaned closer to the slight, dark-haired stranger. The laughter was gone from his face and a snarl twisted his mouth. "If you know what's good for you, you'll keep your trap shut about how those papers got where they are. Understand?"

The teacher came in just then, so quietly

Frank didn't know she was there.

"Franklin!" she exclaimed.

He turned deliberately and straightened Greg thought he caught a note of fear in Frank's eyes, but when he spoke he was loud and intent on showing off. "Yes, Ma'am!"

"What are you doing out of your seat?" she demanded.

He strutted back to his desk and dropped heavily into it. "Let's just pretend that I never left it—shall we?"

Don Gressert snickered and the faint, nervous laughter of a few of his friends rippled uneasily from one row to another. Miss Donnelson looked furious and rapped on her desk with whitened knuckles.

"Franklin!" she exclaimed in exasperation. "Come over here and pick up every one of these papers on Mitzi's desk and on the floor."

Moving tantalizingly slow, he picked a piece of paper off the girl's desk and dropped it in the basket.

"You can move faster than that."

"Can I?" he sneered.

Mark and Don laughed again.

"You're going to pick up every piece of paper if it takes all day."

When he saw that she meant what she said, he went to work and soon filled the basket, then returned it to its place beside Miss Donnelson's desk. He started back to his own seat but she ordered him to the principal's office.

"That doesn't sound like any fun," he said, laughing nervously.

"You heard me!"

He looked about the class, making a face until half the kids were laughing again and Miss Donnelson had trouble quieting them.

"I don't want to hear any more of that kind of talk out of you, Franklin. Go!"

"What if I don't?" he defied her. "Just what'll you do about it?"

"I'll go to Mr. Wagner myself and he'll come after you," she promised him.

"I'm going! I'm going!" He snickered and left the room, mimicking the stiff, arthritic walk of the gray-haired teacher to the vast amusement of the kids. They were in an uproar as he paused in the doorway and again made a face.

Greg didn't know what went on in the principal's office, but he guessed that Frank was really catching it. He didn't come back to the room that period and his desk was empty for the next. Greg wondered if he might have been expelled, but he appeared for his final class, quiet and subdued.

The rest of the week Frank sat sullenly in his seat, without responding to the antics of his new friends or giving any more trouble himself. Greg thought perhaps he had learned his lesson, but he wasn't sure about that. The same cynical hardness marred Frank's features and there was a more pronounced sneer in his voice when he answered a question.

The boys and Kim wanted to go out to the Lazy H the following Saturday to work out for the Little Mavericks' Rodeo, but they weren't sure they would be welcome, the way Frank had been treating them. Greg and Kimberly discussed the matter at the dinner table Friday evening.

"I thought you'd been invited to go out there any Saturday you wanted to," Kevin said.

"We had," Greg replied.

"Then what's the hang-up?"

"Since Frank has been running around with that Don Gressert and Mark Thieben," Kim answered, "we don't know if we're really welcome."

"Besides, Frank's mad at me for calling out at the ranch to see why he wasn't in school the day he ditched," Greg said. "He claims I did it on purpose—to get him in trouble."

"He might not want you to come back out to the ranch," Kevin said, glancing impishly at his sister, "but he wants Kim to come, that's for sure. He *likes* her."

She glared at him and muttered darkly for him to be quiet if he knew what was good for him, but Kevin acted as though he hadn't heard.

"He told me so, Kim. He said that he likes you."

"Kevin Powell!" she exploded. "Don't say *one* more word! Not another word!"

Greg expected his dad to put a stop to the teasing, but before anyone could say anything the phone rang.

"It's Frank," Mrs. Powell said. "He wants to talk to you, Greg."

"Are you sure he doesn't want to talk to Kim?" Kevin asked softly.

Kim looked at him indignantly.

A moment later Greg returned to the table. "Well," he said, "we've got our invitation out to the Lazy H."

Kevin grinned and was about to say something but Kim warned him to silence with her eyes.

The next morning when the three arrived at the Lazy H they thought Mark and Don would be there, but Frank was waiting for them alone. Greg wanted to ask where they were, but didn't dare. Hipolita, however, wasn't so restrained.

"Where're your buddies?" he demanded.

Frank glanced over his shoulder to be sure his uncle and Mr. Powell were not within hearing distance. "Don ditched school last week and got caught," he whispered. "His old man came down on him hard. Grounded him for two whole weeks."

"What about Mark?"

"He was along and got grounded, too."

They got the horses out of the trailer and Mr. Powell drove away.

"I'm sure glad for another chance to try my hand at roping," Greg said, mounting Patches. "I need the practice."

"You're right about that," Frank sneered.

Greg braced himself for more of the same, but the rancher's nephew changed the subject abruptly.

"Uncle Lee and I got the calves up this morning, but I got to thinking that Kim might want to have a go at the barrels first."

Greg and Hip grinned and her cheeks flushed.

"I'll time you, Kim," Frank said. "OK?"

While Greg and Hip watched, Frank planted himself at the line that marked the start-finish of the cloverleaf barrel race. He checked the stopwatch and signaled that he was ready.

Kim drove her heels into the horse's flanks. Patches leaped forward, his hooves pounding the hard arena to the first barrel. He circled it eagerly, so close Greg didn't think he could have put his hand between the hard-running horse's hip and the barrel. It was the same at the second and the third. When Kim and Patches crossed the finish line Frank whistled in amazement.

"24.67 seconds!" he exclaimed. "That's all right! That's great for this early in the season."

"Thanks!" She sat Patches for a moment or two, waiting for his chest to stop heaving.

Frank went over and took hold of the horse's bridle. "I wish you hadn't brought those guys along," he said, keeping his voice down. "You and I could go riding and have a lot of fun."

"I didn't bring them," she announced primly. "They brought me."

"Well, whatever. . . ." He shrugged. "They're here and we've got to put up with it."

"I enjoy having them around," she told him.

He scowled up at her. "You would!"

Greg didn't like what Frank was trying to do and started toward them.

"Here!" Frank exclaimed, shoving the stopwatch into the taller boy's hand. "You time her if you want to. I've got things to do!" He strode away, leaving his guests together in the arena.

9.

Frank Ellis was sullen and morose when he came to school on Monday. He slouched into the sprawling structure and headed for his locker without seeming to notice the students hurrying along the corridors.

Greg spoke to him and their gaze met briefly, but there was no warmth or friendliness in it. Frank pushed by without speaking, as though he had passed a tree or a parking meter. The snub was so obvious that Greg turned to stare after him. He was just in time to see Frank wave to Don and Mark, who had just turned the corner in the hall.

"I can't figure that guy out," a familiar voice at Greg's elbow said. He knew who it was without turning to look.

"Neither can I, Hip."

"He's in for a real burn runnin' around with those Joes. They're bad medicine."

"I know," Greg said, "but try to tell him that."

They covered half the distance to their home room before Hipolita spoke again. "The way Frank treats me," he said at last, "I ought to tell him to hang it in his ear, but I feel sorry for the guy . . . I can't help it."

"Me too."

"I've even got my folks praying for him, but it doesn't seem to do any good. Nothing happens."

Greg had some difficulties with an English

theme that morning and was working so hard on it he didn't think about Frank again until classes were over and they were all heading for the lunchroom. Frank and his pals charged down the hall three abreast, forcing everyone to scatter or be hit.

Greg narrowly avoided being slammed into as they rushed by on their way to the dining hall. They tried to act as though the near collision had been an accident and shouted their apologies, but Greg knew better. It had been deliberate.

"Out of our way!" Don cried boisterously. "Out of our way!"

Frank and his pals pushed through the lunchroom, got their food, and sat at a table nearby. Then, while Greg and Hip moved past in the line, he took three pop bottles from his lunch pail and set them out.

"Hey, guys!" he exclaimed, snickering. "Look who's here!"

"I don't know 'em," Mark blurted, his voice loud and taunting. "I never saw 'em before!"

"Me neither." Frank laughed again. "If I did, we'd share our pop with 'em, wouldn't we?"

"Oh, no!" Don reached out quickly and grasped the bottle in front of him, almost knocking it over.

"I brought it," Frank retorted belligerently. "If I want to give 'em a swallow, I'll give 'em a swallow. OK?"

Don slumped in his chair, pouting.

"These're the cowboys," Frank went on so loudly everyone in that half of the lunchroom could hear him. "They were goin' to come out to the ranch and teach me to rope!"

"We didn't say that," Greg began defensively.

Frank pushed his chair noisily back from the table. "Don't you call me a liar!"

Hip touched his friend on the elbow. "Come on," he said quietly, "let's go find a table."

"Good idea."

Frank put both hands on the table in front of him as though he was going to hoist himself to his feet, but instead he glared at Greg and Hip as they walked away.

"Next time they come out to the Lazy H I'll prove to them and everyone else that they're lyin'. Plenty of people out there heard 'em!"

Greg and his pal found a table some distance away from Frank and his friends. "What's the matter with those characters?" he asked.

Hip shrugged. "I don't know for sure, but I can guess."

Greg's gaze met his. "Go on."

The young Chicano spoke softly. "They sound just like my dad used to when he was spaced out on booze."

"How could that be?"

Hip shrugged. "Search me. But they sure act like it."

Miss Donnelson's English class was held the first period of the afternoon, but she wasn't there. She had gone to Denver to get her eyes examined for new glasses and a senior student from a nearby teacher's college was filling in for her. She was a slight, nervous young woman who probably had never taught before.

The kids saw that she was inexperienced and took advantage of her. They were noisier and more unruly than usual, whispering among themselves and being slow to respond to her directives. Even Greg leaned over and talked to his friend in a low monotone.

Miss Weixel rapped the desk with her ruler. "I must have it quiet!"

"Me, too!" Frank exclaimed, his lips curling. "I'm tired and all this talk keeps me awake."

The others snickered but Don and Mark laughed as though it was the funniest joke they had ever heard.

"Yeah!" Frank repeated. "The noise keeps me awake. Why don't you make 'em be quiet?"

"I'll have no more of that!" She pounded on the desk again with the ruler. "What's your name?"

"I don't have a name. I've got a number!"

"A number!" Don echoed. "That's a good one."

"One more remark out of you and you'll go to the principal's office."

For answer, Frank got to his feet deliberately and started for the door.

"And where do you think you're going?" she demanded.

"To the boys' rest room. That's OK, isn't it?"

She paused. "Come right back."

"Hey, Frank!" Don called as the rancher's nephew went out the door. "Come right back!"

When he returned to his seat some minutes later Frank slouched into it and leaned back, closing his eyes. If Miss Weixel noticed, she

99

gave no sign. At last the bell rang, signaling
that the period was over. She sighed wearily
and watched the students file out to make room
for the next class.

Frank stirred uncertainly at the first sound of
the bell and pushed himself upright, shaking
his head. He fumbled with his books and was
the last to leave the room.

"I think he was actually asleep, Hip," Greg
said as they made their way to their next class.
"Until the bell rang I thought he was faking it,
but now I wonder. There was something weird
about him this afternoon."

Hipolita nodded. "That's what I've been
tryin' to tell you."

Greg had seen guys smashed on liquor before
and he had to admit that Frank and his buddies
sure acted the part. Only he didn't see how they
could get the stuff. They had been in school all
day.

The next two or three days Frank was quiet
and subdued, and so were his friends. For some
reason they seemed to avoid Greg and Hip.

Then the same thing happened again. Frank
and his friends seemed all right during the
morning classes, but in the afternoon they were
loud and boisterous. It started in Miss Donnelson's class when she read off the names of those
who had not handed in their themes when they
were due. All three were on the list.

"Franklin," she said, peering at him through
her new glasses, "I've been going over your
grades. You're slipping badly."

He scowled at her.

"For the last month you've been doing D minus work. Unless you get your theme in by Monday and earn a good grade on it I'll have to turn your name in to the principal."

"So?" His lips curled contemptuously about the word.

"So you'll get a down slip and won't be able to take part in any extracurricular activities."

"Big deal!" he sneered.

She went on to lecture him about the importance of learning to study while he was in junior high and how he should be working hard to get grades that would equal his potential. He listened for a few moments, then put his arms on his desk and rested his head on them. She stopped abruptly.

"Franklin!"

He did not move.

"Franklin!" She rapped on the desk sharply. "Franklin!"

When he didn't move she marched down the aisle and grasped him roughly by the shoulder. "Franklin!" she exclaimed again, shaking him. "Stop this nonsense and sit up and listen to me."

He raised his head deliberately, grimacing at her.

"If you do that once more you're going to Mr. Wagner's office. And that's a promise!"

He straightened slowly, a widening grin twisting his young features. Don and Mark were both chuckling noisily. She whirled and glared at them until they fell silent. That seemed to end the incident.

Bernard Palmer

Walking home from school that afternoon, Greg and Hip talked about the incident.

"There has got to be something wrong!" Greg said. "A guy just doesn't fall asleep that easy."

"There is something wrong," Hip said firmly. "Those guys are hittin' the booze. My dad used to fall asleep that way when he was drunk."

Greg shifted his books from one arm to the other thoughtfully. What Hip said was probably true. After all, he had seen a lot of drinking around his home before his dad got his life straightened out and quit the booze.

"We can't squeal on them," Greg said, "but we've got to do something to stop them."

Hip shrugged expressively. "Like what?"

"I don't know." Greg stopped at the street corner to allow a cattle truck to go by. "The first thing, I suppose, is to get real proof that they're drinking in school."

Hip faced him. "I already know that."

"But we've got to have proof."

"Then what?" the young Chicano asked. "What are we going to do after we get the proof you say we've got to have?"

Greg hadn't thought about that. "We'll have to think of something."

They decided, first, to keep their eyes open and spot anything else that was unusual in the way Frank and his pals acted. They arranged to get to school a little earlier than usual and hang around the halls.

For several days they could see no definite pattern. One day the three would be quiet and almost courteous in the morning, then become loud and unruly in the afternoon. When that happened, Greg and Hip tried to get close enough to smell their breath, but the guys were adept at keeping away from them.

Then, for a couple of days nothing out of the ordinary happened and Greg and Hip began to get discouraged. They began to think they would never get the evidence they needed to prove what Frank, Mark and Don were doing.

Greg was confident that he and Hip were being so secretive that no one, aside from themselves, knew what they were doing. However, near home one evening Kevin and a friend accosted Greg and Hip and demanded to know what was going on.

"What do you mean?" the older brother asked evasively.

"You know. What're you and Hip doin' out at school? What're you tryin' to find out?" He lowered his voice. "You can trust us. We won't squeal on you. What're you guys doin'?"

"Studying."

"That's not what I mean." He was exasperated and let Greg know it. "Tommie's older brother said that you're both prowlin' up and down the halls like a pair of private eyes on TV. What gives?"

Greg grinned crookedly but said nothing.

"We'll find out somehow. And when we do we're liable to blab it all over the place—unless you let us in on it."

Greg grasped his arm, squeezing it in warning. "If you don't want to get clobbered, you'll keep your mouth shut."

Kevin pulled away. "Let us in on it and we'll keep still. We know how to keep a secret, don't we, Tommie?"

"You'll keep quiet, anyway, if you know what's good for you—and you too, Tommie." Greg squeezed Kevin's arm harder until his younger brother yelped with pain.

"I won't tell anybody! I won't tell anybody!"

"Neither will I," Tommie assured them.

Kimberly came along about then, in time to hear her younger brother's frantic statement. "You'll be quiet about what?" she asked.

"I—"

"It's nothing that would concern you," Greg broke in.

She moved closer. "Then why don't you tell us what you and Hip are doing when you go to school so early every morning?"

He glared at her. "It just so happens that it doesn't concern either of you." Before they could press for more information Greg and Hip turned away from them, hurried into the house and to the privacy of Greg's room.

"Now what do we do?" Hip asked, scarcely mouthing the words. "How do we keep them from finding out?"

"Easy. We don't tell them anything. Not a single thing."

"They'll keep at us," he said. "At least my brothers would. They'd be on my back day and night until they got some answers."

"They may keep at us but we'll keep our mouths shut. They won't find out a thing."

The following Sunday Mr. Huffman pulled

into the Powell yard with Frank at the usual time and the boy rode over to the church with the family in the station wagon. However, he hung back as the others went inside.

"Come on," Greg told him, "or we'll be late."

"You go ahead."

"Come on."

"I've got something else to do this morning for a little while."

Greg was about to question him further when he saw Mark and Don on the sidewalk across the street.

"I—I'm goin' over to talk to the guys for a minute," the rancher's nephew said defensively. "I—I'll be there in a jiffy."

Greg frowned. "I'll bet!"

"Listen!" Frank warned, cocking his fist. "If you say a word to my Uncle Lee—one word—about my not bein' in Sunday school this morning, I'll teach you a lesson you won't forget."

"You and who else?" Greg asked, amused at the fact that Frank who was so much smaller than he, was threatening him.

"If I have to have help," the other boy promised in guarded tones, "I can get it. I've got friends!"

10.

Bernard Palmer

Greg thought perhaps Frank would come into the Sunday school class a few minutes late, after talking to his friends, but there was no sign of him. Between services he went out on the front steps and looked around, but Frank was not in sight. When church was over, however, Frank came up beside Greg on the sidewalk in front of the building.

"Great sermon, wasn't it?" he asked, grinning.

"How would you know?"

"What do you mean, how would I know?" he demanded. "I was there. Don't you remember? I sat right beside you."

"You know better than that."

"I was." His voice tensed ominously. "And if you know what's good for you, you'll not lie to that uncle of mine about my not being in Sunday school and church this morning."

"If he asks me," Greg said, "he's going to get the truth."

"Don't you lie about me or you'll have to answer to me and my friends!"

Mr. Huffman pulled up and stopped for his nephew just then, waving to Greg and Hip. They waved back.

"Man," Hip said when the other boy was gone, "if Mr. Huffman only knew that Frank wasn't here for services, he'd clobber him. Makin' him

drive all that way into town just so he could go
to Sunday school and church and then have
him sneak out that way."

Greg's friend turned to watch the Lazy H
pickup pull away from the curb and move down
the street toward the highway. "My dad'd give
me a good tannin' if I pulled anything like that
on him and he ever found out about it."

"So would mine."

The corners of Hip's mouth tightened. "Are
you goin' to keep still like he warned us to?"

Greg Powell pulled in a deep breath. The fact
that Frank had threatened him if he told was
enough to make him want to do it, just to let the
guy know that he wasn't afraid of him and his
friends. But there was something that kept him
from doing so. He just couldn't squeal on the
guy.

"I don't think we'll have to tell on him. If he
keeps it up, his uncle's going to get wise, sooner
or later. He'll catch Frank on the street or
something."

But Hip was not so sure. "Maybe he will and
maybe he won't. The guy's pretty slick."

"Not that slick. You wait and see. He'll give
himself away."

The following day the boys were walking to
school together, leaving home a few minutes
before Kim and Kevin were ready, when they
saw Frank near the school. He wasn't heading
for the building with the other kids, however. He
walked around the rear of the school bus and
made his way across the street toward an alley.

"Look," Hip said, indicating the rancher's

nephew with a quick gesture. "There goes Frank. I'll bet he's goin' to ditch again this morning."

But Greg was not so sure. "I saw Don and Mark heading for that same alley not two minutes ago."

"Maybe all three of them are going to skip out for the day."

"Let's follow him and see."

"Follow him?" Hipolita echoed, his eyes widening. "In bright daylight? How're we goin' to do that without gettin' caught?"

"Keep quiet and come along with me. I'll show you."

"I still don't see how—"

"Just do as you're told and don't talk."

It was obvious that Hip wasn't satisfied with Greg's assurance that they would not be seen, but he did as he was told. They cut diagonally across the street, being careful to keep to Frank's back and some distance away from him. The house on the corner had a garage at the alley and a high hedge running from the back inside corner to the neighbor's lot line. They made for the frame garage, ducked into the yard in front of it, and moved cautiously toward the hedge.

"She's watchin' us from the kitchen window," Hip whispered tensely in his companion's ear.

"Who's watching us?"

"Mrs. Swanstrom. We'd better get out of here! You know how she yells if anybody steps on her lawn."

"Just a minute." Greg put a finger to his lips

in warning and tiptoed forward, half a step at a time.

They were nearing the place in the alley where Frank's friends had been waiting for him, with only the hedge between them. Greg stopped, crouching cautiously. His best friend moved up behind him uneasily.

"Did you get it?" they heard Don ask in a whisper.

"I said I would, didn't I?"

"How much?"

"A liter. That's the way Uncle Lee buys it."

"Where's the 7-Up?"

"Right here."

"Good! Help me get this stuff in the bottles so we can get back to school. The bell's goin' to ring any second."

Greg inched forward and parted the thick hedge slightly to see what the trio in the alley was doing. Mark poured part of the contents of two 7-Up bottles into a third empty bottle and held them out for Frank. He removed a fancy shaped glass container from his lunch pail and began to fill the pop bottles to the neck with the clear, colorless liquid. *Vodka,* the label proclaimed.

It was all Greg could do to keep from gasping aloud. Hip was right! Frank and his friends were drinking in school. The rancher's nephew was stealing vodka from Mr. Huffman's bar at home. It was one alcoholic beverage that had but little odor. They could mix it with pop and drink it right in the lunchroom with little chance of getting caught.

Greg glanced at Hip who was grinning triumphantly, as though to say, I told you so. They were still staring at each other when there was a sudden squeaking noise from the house behind them. A window was being pushed up and a strident feminine voice shouted, "You out there! What're you doing?"

"Who's that?" Frank cried in a hoarse whisper.

"Whatever you're doing, stop right now or I'll call the police!"

"Come on!" he said weakly. "We've got to get out of here!"

"She can't do a thing to us," Mark blustered. "This is a public alley. She doesn't own it."

"Maybe not, but I don't want to be caught anyway!" Frank dropped the bottle into his lunch pail and the three of them dashed in the direction of the school.

On the other side of the hedge Greg and his friend straightened and turned around.

"We're in big trouble now," Hip murmured. "She's mean. She'll call the cops for sure."

Greg motioned for him to be quiet. Fortunately for them, the guys in the alley had been so frightened at the sound of the woman's voice that they had dashed away without realizing that old Mrs. Swanstrom hadn't been able to see them. If they had thought they would have realized that there had to have been someone on the other side of the hedge and that they were being spied on. All of that Greg considered as he moved forward, smiling.

"Gregory Powell!" Mrs. Swanstrom exclaimed when he drew close enough for her to recognize him. "What were you doing in my yard?"

"Some guys from school were in the alley and we wanted to see what they were doing," he told her.

"Land sakes," she continued. "You should have let me know first. I might have called the police on you."

He apologized for not letting her know who he was and what he and Hip were doing.

"Well," she said, "there was no harm done. Come in and have some cookies and hot chocolate and see Princess and Geronimo."

They had to turn down the snack because it was almost time for the tardy bell to ring. Greg apologized again and they hurried toward the school building.

"So that's why you didn't pay any attention when I told you someone was watching us from the window," Hip said. "But what gives? Who are Geronimo and Princess?"

"They're her cats. We take care of them when she goes out to California to visit her son," Greg replied. "And anybody who's a friend of her cats is a friend of hers."

"I wish I'd known that when we were in her yard. I was so scared I just about passed out when that window went up and she started yelling at us."

Just inside the school building Hip paused momentarily. "Well, we got our proof like you wanted," he said. "Now what do we do?"

Greg shook his head. "I haven't figured that

out yet."

"When you do," Hip said, "let me know."

Greg was still pondering the matter when he got home that night. He sat in the family room alone staring at the cold fireplace. That was where he was when his dad joined him.

"What're you doing, Greg?" Mr. Powell asked. "Don't you have any homework?"

"A little." He looked up uneasily. "Hip and I have got a big problem and we don't know what to do about it."

"You aren't in any trouble, are you?"

"Oh, no," he said quickly. "It's nothing like that." He shifted his position uneasily. He felt that he had to talk to his dad about it, to get his advice. Yet he couldn't tell him who was involved or what the guys were doing that disturbed him and Hip so much.

"Would you like to talk about it?" Mr. Powell asked. He sat down on the raised hearth and leaned back against the stone fireplace front.

"Hip and I got concerned about these friends—these guys we know," he began. "They were acting so—so strange that we were afraid they were doing something they shouldn't be doing. So we've sort of been snooping around."

"I see." His frown deepened. "And I suppose you found out something you wish you hadn't."

"That's about it."

There was a long silence. "Is there anything more that you want to tell me?"

"I guess not," Greg said. "Our problem is— what do we do now?"

"And this is something that's really bad. Is

that it?"

He nodded almost imperceptibly.

"And you don't want to squeal on them. Is that the way it is?"

"I *can't* squeal on them, Dad!" Greg exclaimed in desperation. "You know what everyone at school would think of me if I did!"

His father took a long while in answering. "I can understand the problem you've got, and frankly, I admire your loyalty. But there is another side to this. If you don't do something they're going to keep right on and the next time it will get worse. You've got an obligation to try and help them."

"I know. But how?"

"You owe it to them to talk to them about it."

"What?" he demanded, startled by the suggestion. That was one thing he could never do.

"It's this way. If they learn that you and Hip found out what they're doing, they're going to realize that other people will find out before long. They'll know they're not getting away with anything."

Hurt leaped into Greg's eyes. "But Dad!" he protested.

"I know it won't be easy."

Greg got to his feet and stared beyond his father. He clenched his fists until his knuckles whitened. He had talked to his dad because he thought he could help him. He had never supposed he would suggest something like this.

Mr. Powell understood the anguish his son was experiencing. "It's not going to be easy,

Greg," he repeated, "but you've asked my advice and I've given it to you. The only other alternative that I can see would be to go to their parents or the principal."

"But Dad!" he angrily exploded again.

"You owe it to those boys to do something, Greg. You can't hide your head in the sand and pretend that this thing didn't happen. If you keep quiet, in a way you will be as guilty as they are."

He tried once more to make his father understand. "But this will ruin me! I won't have a friend at school—except Hip. And if I get him involved by going to those guys, he might get so mad at me that he won't speak to me again either!"

Mr. Powell put a reassuring hand on his son's shoulder. "Mother and I will be praying for you that you'll make the right decision," he said.

11.

Bernard Palmer

Greg went to his room that night soon after the family got up from the dinner table. He tried to study but could not put his mind to it. The words shimmered on the page and he found himself reading the same paragraph over and over again without understanding it. He was having a quiz in the morning but he just wasn't able to apply himself the way he usually did.

His dad could talk about going to Frank if he wanted to. It was easy for him. He wouldn't have to do it. But Greg knew what would happen if he followed his dad's advice. That character wouldn't be listening to what he said. He'd be trying to figure some way of getting Greg to be quiet about what he and Hip had seen. Don and Mark were in on it, too. Frank would probably get them on his back in an effort to make him keep his mouth shut.

Not that he was afraid of them. He knew them well enough to know that they would back off if he and Hip stood up to them. He wasn't even concerned that they might catch him alone. They bragged a lot about all the things they would do, but they were short on action. It was the talking to Frank that upset him. His throat went dry just thinking about it.

He pushed away from his desk and stood without quite knowing why. How could he talk to a guy like Frank about his drinking? Frank

118

wouldn't think there was anything wrong with it. It was all a big joke and his only concern would be not getting caught.

He went over to the window where he remained motionless for several minutes, talking to God about the problem. He tried to recall all the reasons he could think of for not following his dad's advice, but the more he tried to justify remaining silent, the more convicted he became. Finally he quit fighting and gave in.

"Dear God," he prayed quietly, "I don't want to talk to Frank. I don't think he'll listen to me and I don't see that any good could come of it, but I know that You want me to follow Dad's advice. So, I'm going to. But I—I'll have to have Your help or I'll get things fouled up worse than they are now."

He thought he would feel better after that. In a way he did since he knew what he had to do. As long as he thought about his dad's advice and the fact that he was sure God wanted him to follow it, he was all right. But when he thought about Frank and what it would be like to tell him that he knew what he and his pals were doing, cold sweat broke out on his forehead and an icy emptiness gripped his stomach. It wasn't going to be easy. In fact, he was sure it would be the hardest thing he had ever done in his life.

The next morning when Greg got up he wondered if he felt well enough to go to school. He had a headache and was queasy and uncomfortable. He looked at his face in the bathroom mirror and ran his hand over his smooth young cheek. If he were honest with

Bernard Palmer

himself he had to admit that his sickness was
not physical but came from what he had to do
that morning. It was a coward's way of getting
out of something unpleasant. Grimly he forced
himself to go into the kitchen, eat breakfast
with the family, and head for school.

He knew he should talk to Hip about what he
was going to do. His pal was in on it, too, and
should have something to say about what they
did. The truth was, Greg admitted to himself, he
didn't trust his own courage. He already knew
what God would have him do. He had battled it
out the night before, but he was so timorous
about it he was afraid that any opposition or
doubt from Hip would be enough to cause him to
change his mind. He couldn't risk that.

He found Frank in the hall and told him that
he had to talk to him.

"Can't it wait?" he demanded irritably. "I've
got something else to do right now."

"No, it can't wait," Greg blurted. "I've got to
talk to you."

"This morning?"

"Right away."

"What about?" Suspicion crept into his voice.

"About what I saw." Greg looked around.
"Let's go where we've got a little more privacy."

Frank shrugged indifferently and followed
Greg out the front door and to one side of the
building, away from the flow of traffic. "Now,
what's this big deal that's got you so uptight
you can't wait 'til noon to talk to me about it?"

Greg's fists flexed nervously. Talking to the
other boy was even more difficult than he had

120

anticipated. But he had started, he had to go through with it.

"It's what we—I mean what I saw a few days ago in the alley behind Mrs. Swanstrom's."

Frank's cheeks went ashen and his lower lip quivered. "I don't know what you're talkin' about."

"I think you do. The vodka you guys put in your pop bottles."

Anger flared in Frank's eyes and they narrowed ominously. "You don't know what you're talkin' about," he snarled in a voice little above a whisper. "And you'd better not spread that story around if you know what's good for you."

"It won't do any good to lie. I saw you pour part of the 7-Up from two bottles into a third. Then you took a vodka bottle from your lunch pail and filled the three bottles with it."

"You don't expect anyone to believe that lie, do you?"

But Greg was not to be stopped. "I could hear you. You said it was from your Uncle Lee's private stock."

Frank was visibly shaken. "You tell that to anyone," he blustered, "and Don and Mark and I'll get you for it!"

"You can quit sweating it," Greg said. "I'm not going to rat on you."

"Now you're soundin' halfway smart."

"Cool it, Frank. I'm not squealin' on you, and I'm not afraid of you, either."

"You'd better be afraid of us. The three of us stand together. If someone has trouble with one of us, he has got to take care of all of us!"

"Come off it," Greg continued. "I'm just trying to pound some sense into you. You've got to shape up. You're not goin' to get away with drinking much longer, and when you do get caught you'll be in big trouble."

Frank relaxed slightly and laughed at his companion. "I know what I'm doin'," he said. "You let me worry about gettin' into trouble. OK?"

"You'd better start. Somebody's goin' to wise up before long. And when they do, the roof's goin' to fall in."

"See you around," Frank smirked.

Greg watched until he was out of sight. He had talked with Frank so he should have felt better, but he didn't. It hadn't done any good at all. He even began to wonder if he had been mistaken in thinking God wanted him to approach Frank about his drinking. It all seemed so useless.

For the rest of the week Greg saw nothing unusual in the behavior of Frank and his friends that would indicate that they were drinking again. They spoke to him when they met in the halls, but that was all. And when Sunday came, Frank didn't show up at the Powell place to go to church. Mrs. Huffman phoned shortly before 9:30 to tell them that he was ill.

"It sounds to me as though it's a special kind of sickness," Hip said upon learning why Frank hadn't come that morning. They met before Sunday school beside the Rodriguez car in the church parking lot.

"What do you mean?" Greg asked.

"Being sick goes with drinking—especially if a guy gets drunk."

Greg nodded as though in agreement, but he wondered if his friend was right about the reason for Frank's staying home. It could be the conversation he'd had with him outside the school building Friday morning.

On Monday Greg saw the rancher's nephew in the corridor before class. He spoke to him but Frank pushed by without answering. That didn't bother Greg, however. He shoved his thoughts about Frank to the inner recesses of his mind until that afternoon when one of the boys in his grade burst back into Miss Donnelson's English class the first period after lunch.

"Somethin' weird's goin' on in the boys' bathroom!" he cried. "Frank Ellis is layin' on the floor and can't get up!"

"Greg!" Miss Donnelson ordered crisply. "Hurry and get Mr. Wagner! Have him go in and see about Franklin."

He got the principal and rushed into the boys' rest room half a step behind Mr. Wagner. Frank lay motionless on the floor. His face was white and drawn, and his eyes were closed.

"Frank!" the principal said, bending over him. "Can you hear me?"

The boy moved slightly and his eyelids fluttered.

"Is he all right?" Greg asked, concern tearing at him.

The principal looked up. "Go to my office and

have my secretary phone Dr. Lambert to come out right away."

"What's wrong?"

Mr. Wagner did not answer his question. "The doctor will be here in a few minutes. Wait for him at the front door and bring him here."

The next few moments were a blur to Greg. He remembered rushing back to the principal's office and repeating Mr. Wagner's order to his secretary. And he went to the door fearfully to wait for the doctor, a prayer surging in his heart.

Whatever was wrong with Frank, it had to be something serious. He was unconscious, or nearly so. Greg thought about his own attitude toward the rancher's nephew and was stricken for it. He had been praying that Frank would confess his sin and receive Christ as his Saviour, but Greg hadn't really been burdened for him. He hadn't been concerned enough to give that an important place in his priorities. If he was to be completely honest, he would have to admit that he had really been praying for Frank out of duty and not because it mattered deeply to him.

The doctor parked as close to the front door of the school as possible and hurried in.

"This way!" Greg sprinted down the corridor ahead of him and whipped into the boys' rest room. He didn't know whether or not he was supposed to go inside, but he did.

The doctor knelt beside the inert figure on the floor, pulled back Frank's eyelid and checked his pulse. Then he bent closer and smelled the boys' breath.

"Is it what I think it is?" Mr. Wagner wanted to know.

Dr. Lambert nodded. "Vodka, I would guess. All I can smell is the alcohol, but he's drunk."

"I thought so. He must have had a load of the stuff."

"He's not very big. It would hit him much harder than it would a full-grown man. The same amount of liquor, I mean."

The two men loaded Frank into the doctor's car and drove him to the hospital. Greg didn't know how the story of Frank being drunk got out so rapidly. He didn't think he had said anything to anyone about it, but he had been so confused and bewildered during those first awful minutes that he couldn't be sure. However it had happened, by the time they were dismissed from classes that afternoon practically everyone in the building knew about it.

The kids also knew that Greg and Hip had been friendly with Frank and took delight in talking with them about him.

"Did you know that the janitor found an empty vodka bottle in the wastebasket of the boys' rest room?" one of the guys asked Greg.

He hadn't heard that before, he replied. And what was more, he didn't want to talk about it.

12.

At school the next day Greg learned that Frank was going to be released from the hospital the following morning. He also learned that the rancher's nephew was in serious trouble.

"If I were him," the son of a school board member said knowingly, "I'd want to stay in the hospital as long as I could. My dad said that they called his uncle in and talked with him. Frank got his liquor out at the Lazy H and Mr. Huffman is mad enough to tear him apart."

"Don and Mark aren't having it all that easy, either," someone else put in. "I saw them go into Mr. Wagner's office this morning before school and they were still there two hours later. Their folks were here and everything."

"Yeah, I think all three are going to get expelled."

Greg knew the boys deserved whatever they got in the way of punishment for drinking. Still, it disturbed him. He couldn't understand why so many at school were almost gleeful about it. Some even acted as though it was a big joke.

On Tuesday night at family devotions George Powell brought up the subject. He told the family that Mr. Huffman had been in to see him at the newspaper office that afternoon.

"I suppose he wanted to try to get the paper to kill the story," Christine Powell said.

Her husband shook his head. "As a matter of fact, the subject didn't even come up. He's furious with Frank for getting into his liquor cabinet. He claims that he always keeps it locked, but his nephew found where he keeps the key and started raiding it."

"Did you remind him that he shouldn't have had liquor around the house at all?"

"I didn't have the chance. I'll have to talk with him about that later. It wouldn't have done any good to mention it to him this afternoon. He was so mad all he could think about was punishing Frank."

"Did they expel him?" Greg asked.

"The school authorities finally decided to let the boys attend classes on probation. They won't be able to take part in any outside activities, and if they cause trouble of any kind—are caught drinking again or let their grades fall—they'll be expelled for the rest of the school year."

"That's rough."

"I know it is, Greg, but what they have done is very serious." He picked up the Bible and opened it to the portion of Scripture they would be reading.

"Mr. Huffman also said that he has forbidden Frank to have Don and Mark out at the ranch again. He's not even supposed to associate with them. He told Mr. Wagner if he sees Frank with either Don or Mark, he wants him expelled."

"Wow!" Kevin exclaimed. "That blows the Little Mavericks' Rodeo as far as those two are concerned."

Bernard Palmer

"It blows it for Frank, too. Mr. Huffman isn't going to let him compete."

When they finished reading the Bible passage that night they had special prayer. Most of it was devoted to Frank and his pals. They prayed that God would help the trio learn their lesson and not drink anymore, and that they would receive Christ as their Saviour.

Frank wasn't at school the next morning, but he did come in at noon. Greg happened to be at his locker nearby when Don and Mark approached the rancher's nephew.

"Hey, man! It's good to see you," Don said. "That was a bummer!"

"You sure tied on a good one!" Mark snickered. "I'll bet your head felt as big as a basketball."

Frank retreated several paces. "I can't be around you guys," he told them.

"How's your uncle to know?" Mark demanded.

"I'm supposed to be expelled if Mr. Wagner sees us together."

"That's gross!"

There was a slight sound behind him and Frank glanced quickly over his shoulder, as though expecting his uncle to come striding through the door and catch him talking to Don and Mark.

"What about the rodeo Saturday?"

"It's off for you guys. Uncle Lee won't let you on the place."

"But we've already entered the calf riding, breakaway roping and goat tying."

130

"We've been working out all spring," Don countered. "It's not fair to keep us from competing now."

"Besides, it's the state Little Mavericks' Rodeo. It's not up to your uncle who can enter."

"Maybe not, but it's up to him who comes on the Lazy H Ranch."

"I think I'll come anyway," Mark blustered. "He can't shove us around."

Frank shuddered. "Have you ever seen Uncle Lee when he's real mad?"

The other boy shook his head.

"Let me clue you. You'd better stay out of his way. I wouldn't be within 50 miles of him when he's mad if I could help it."

At that point Don Gressert saw Greg at his locker. "This is all *your* fault," he said accusingly.

Greg did not answer him.

"You squealed on us."

"No way. You squealed on yourselves."

Mr. Wagner appeared at the far end of the corridor just then and Frank turned quickly, fumbling with the locker in front of him.

"You can't get in that one," Greg said, trying to sound warm and friendly.

"I don't know why not . . . if I can just get the key in the lock."

"That's the trouble. You're trying the wrong locker. The key won't fit."

Frank took half a step backward and looked up at the number. His cheeks flamed with embarrassment. Deliberately he turned to Greg. "I'm going to make you a promise," he muttered darkly. "I'm goin' to get even with you for what you did."

"But I didn't do anything except talk to you," Greg protested.

"Don't try to tell me that. You talked to Mr. Wagner about me. That's how he found out."

"You know better than that."

Frank ignored Greg's protest of innocence. "Just remember, I'm gettin' even! I don't know how or when, but I'm warnin' you right now. I'm getting back at you for what you did to me and my buddies."

"If that's the way you feel about it," Greg said indifferently, "there's nothing I can do."

"You'll be sorry you squealed on us!" he exclaimed, poking Greg in the stomach with his forefinger.

Greg saw him around school after that but Frank looked past him or around him, as though he wasn't even there.

"I don't see how he can blame you for his getting caught drinking," Hip said on the way home from school Friday evening. "He was so drunk he had passed out when Ray found him. It wasn't your fault."

Greg Powell shrugged. "Well, I'm not going to worry about it."

When Greg got home from school Kim had taken Patches to the fairgrounds for a last-minute workout with the barrels before the next day's rodeo. She had bribed Kevin into going along to time her by letting him ride Sawdust.

"Oh, Greg!" she said at the supper table an hour or more later, "I'm so excited. You should've been there. I had the best time I've ever had! Twenty-one seconds flat."

He glanced at their younger brother and winked. "Maybe Kevin made a mistake," he teased.

"No way," Kevin said.

"Honest," she went on, "my time was great. I knew that, even before he told me what it was. Everything went perfect."

"Let's hope it goes that way for you in the race tomorrow."

"You'll pray for me, won't you?" she exclaimed. "I'm so excited I don't think I'll be able to sleep at all tonight."

The following morning the entire family went out to the Lazy H. George Powell, Greg and Hip went in the pickup pulling the horse trailer, and Christine took Kim and Kevin in the station wagon. A large crowd had already gathered when the Powells pulled in and unloaded the horses.

"I'm glad you got here on time, George," Lee Huffman said. "I was beginning to wonder whether you were going to make it in time for the first events."

"I wouldn't miss it."

"Well, I hope you get the pictures you want."

It was a bright, warm day and George got out his camera and set to work almost immediately. Frank came over to where he and Greg and Hip were standing near the arena.

"You're going to miss the best shots, Mr. Powell," he said with affected carelessness.

Question leaped to Mr. Powell's eyes.

Bernard Palmer

"I decided not to enter today—to give the other guys a chance." He managed to laugh. "It wouldn't be very friendly of me to have the Little Mavericks' Rodeo out here and then win everything myself now would it?"

Mr. Powell eyed him thoughtfully but made no comment. For a brief instant Greg was irritated. He wanted to tell Frank not to let that stop him, but his dad's eyes warned him to remain silent. To say anything right then would have been unkind. The other boy was lying in a desperate effort to make himself look good. He was trying to hide the fact that his Uncle Lee had forbidden him to take part in the rodeo.

The announcer broke into his thoughts at that point. "The Colorado Little Mavericks' Rodeo is about to get under way. All contestants assemble for the Grand Entry!" he sang over the loudspeaker.

"Hey," one of the spectators near the Powells said to his wife, "this rodeo is right uptown. I can see why they decided to have it out here."

Greg smiled as he started for his horse. They didn't know that his dad was there to photograph the rodeo for his *Western World* article.

He was about to mount Patches when he thought of Kim. Since they were both using the same horse, she wouldn't have a mount to ride in the Grand Entry.

"Kim!" he called. "Come here and ride Patches."

She shook her head. "He's your horse."

"I'll watch."

134

She took the reins and put one foot in the stirrup. By the eager way she took charge of his horse he knew she really wanted to be in the parade, but she did not mount. "I really shouldn't."

"Go ahead."

"You can ride Blaze," Mr. Huffman broke in, approaching them from behind.

Greg looked in the direction of the ranch owner's voice and saw him standing at Blaze's head, his hand on the bridle. His nephew was in the saddle.

"Frank isn't riding today," he said coldly.

"But Uncle Lee!" Frank protested. "This is just the Grand Entry! That won't hurt anything!"

"You should have thought of that before."

The boy dismounted sullenly.

"You'd just as well ride Blaze," Mr. Huffman said to Greg. "You'll get a chance to be in your dad's pictures."

Leading his horse, Frank approached Greg. "Just remember what I told you," he muttered under his breath. "I'm gettin' even with you! You'll find out that you can't shove *me* around!"

Greg mounted Blaze and reined him into the line of riders. He didn't see why the other boy had to blame him for everything. He hadn't caused the trouble.

When the Grand Entry was over and the saddle bronc riding was announced, Greg climbed upon the wooden fence beside Hip and Kim to watch. The first contestant was the son of one of the Lazy H hands. He drew a tough horse and had difficulty staying in the saddle for the full eight seconds. His score was fair but not outstanding. The next was a rider whose dad owned a neighboring spread. He did a little better. The next was Mac Lambert.

"Hey, that's Doc Lambert's kid, isn't it?" Greg asked Hip.

His Chicano friend nodded. "That's him. He can really ride."

The doctor's son had drawn the hardest bucking horse of the string and turned in a ride that brought a round of applause from the people who were watching.

When the first section of the saddle bronc riding was over the calf riding began.

"Think we ought to try it?" Hip asked, glancing hopefully at Greg.

"We entered," he acknowledged uncertainly.

"That's what I was thinking. We'd better get down there in case we're called first."

Greg still hesitated. "I—I've never ridden a calf before."

"There's nothing to it."

"I suppose that's why so many guys get bucked off."

Hip laughed. "That's the worst that can happen."

"I wouldn't say that."

Reluctantly Greg followed his friend down to the chute where the calves were held. Frank saw them leave the fence and followed them. He grasped Greg by the arm. "Where do you think you're going?"

Greg gestured toward the chute.

"Don't tell me that you're going to ride a calf!" he said contemptuously.

"We're both entered," Hip broke in.

"You'd better think a couple of times before you go through with it." His lips curled bitterly.

Greg might not have taken his turn in the calf riding had it not been for the contempt in the other boy's eyes. He certainly couldn't say that he wanted to. But he couldn't back down either. Not to a guy like Frank.

"How about it?" the chute master asked. "Are you going to take your ride or aren't you?"

Moistening his lips with the tip of his tongue, Greg nodded.

He thought he was to ride first, but he was mistaken. Hip was up on a small, wiry calf. It came out of the chute like a cannonball when the gate was swung open. The calf ran to the center of the arena, bucked three or four times, whirled and ran again. When the whistle blew signaling the end of the ride, Hip dismounted effortlessly.

"Hey! You did all right," Greg exclaimed when he came back to the chute.

Two other riders took their turns before Greg was up. When the chute master told him it was his ride, he pulled the heavy leather glove on his right hand.

"You c'n back out, you know," Frank taunted.

Greg turned his back to him and climbed up on the chute, his gaze fixed on the calf he was going to ride. The young bull was big and powerfully built, a shaggy, broad-chested animal that looked as mean as his older brothers. Greg hesitated a moment before lowering himself on the calf's back.

"Did anybody tell you that he has never been ridden?" the rancher's nephew asked.

"Until today," Hip put in loyally. "You're going to see him ridden this morning."

"You think Greg can stay with him? That's a laugh!"

Greg had to agree with Frank. He wondered why he had been so stupid as to let himself get into such a mess. But it was too late! He wondered what it would be like to get bucked off on his head or have a calf walk on his arm.

Frank's laughter rang out. "I hope you haven't forgotten how to pray," he said. "You're goin' to need it now."

"Ready?" the chute master asked.

He tightened his grip on the rope and waved his left hand. The gate swung open and the calf exploded into the arena in one mighty, stiff-legged leap. Shock waves surged up Greg's spine as the animal hit the hard ground with his hooves, but miraculously the boy stayed on board. The calf spun to the right and jumped again, twisting savagely.

Greg felt himself loosen slightly and tightened his grip. The arena spun and whirled before his eyes as the calf threw himself in wild abandon, trying desperately to lose the creature that was on his back. The whistle blew and a cheer went up but Greg continued to ride for three or four jumps. He had forgotten to ask anyone how to get off without tearing his arm from its socket! Then gingerly he loosed his hand and the rope began to slip through his fingers. The instant he felt it at his finger tips he leaped mightily, throwing himself to one side. Somehow he landed standing up and dashed frantically for the fence, to the cheers of the spectators.

"A great ride!" the announcer bawled into the loudspeaker. "Seventy-seven points. That's going to be the ride to beat today!"

"I thought you were afraid to ride a calf," Hip said when he was back at the chute.

"You were just lucky!" Frank Ellis said. "You drew an easy calf."

"You know better'n that," Hip protested. "He's goin' to win!"

Frank snorted. "He wouldn't if I was entered!" With that he turned to Greg. "You're lucky I'm not ridin'. That's all I can tell you. If I was you wouldn't have a chance!"

13.

The rodeo was stopped at noon for a barbeque provided by Lee Huffman and his wife and the next event was not started again until after two o'clock. People had finished eating long before, but they stood around in small groups visiting until the announcer's voice came over the loudspeaker.

"There are some bareback riders in the arena rarin' to go, ladies and gentlemen," he began. "If you don't get over there right away, you'll miss some of the action. . . ."

The spectators began to drift toward the stands and the contestants went to their horses. Greg and Hip wanted to watch the bareback riding, but there wasn't time. Breakaway roping was next and they had to get ready for it.

The boys mounted and rode back to the calf chute where the hand in charge of the rodeo came over to them.

"Sorry," he said, "but we're having trouble with the calves. We're holding the barrel race next."

"Hey!" Greg exclaimed. "I'd better get that sister of mine. That's her event and she's riding my horse."

The arena master glanced at the notebook in his hand. "That's a good idea. Kim Powell's first up."

While the bronc riders continued their event

Greg tied Patches to the arena fence and went to look for his sister. Coming back with her moments later, he saw Frank Ellis standing beside Patches. For a brief instant his temper flared and he quickened his pace.

"What's the rush?" Kim asked, hurrying in an effort to keep up with him. "The bronc riding isn't over yet."

Frank moved away as he saw Greg approaching. The Powell boy stood for a moment beside his horse, checking the saddle and bridle. Satisfied at last that all was in order, he loosed the reins and held them while Kim mounted.

"I don't like to ride Patches before your calf roping, Greg," she said nervously. "I don't want him to be winded when you have to ride him."

"Don't worry. He'll have a chance to catch his breath before I take my turn."

Her eyelids narrowed uneasily. "Maybe I shouldn't race today."

"I don't know why not. You've got the best horse in the race and the best brother rooting for you." His grin was reassuring.

He loosed his hold on Patches. "Well . . . good luck."

She smiled warmly and tightened the reins. "I'm going to need it."

The last bareback rider was getting down on his horse in the chute when Greg and Hip left the far end of the arena where the barrel race would start and finish, and made their way to a point beyond the first barrel.

"She's awful scared," Hip said.

Greg nodded. "It's her first real race. She'll

settle down all right."

They were still talking when Frank came over to them. "What happened to you guys?" he demanded. "Did you decide it wouldn't do you any good to enter the breakaway roping?"

Greg grinned crookedly. "No way. We just came down here so we'd have a good place to watch the barrel race."

"Barrel race?" Frank echoed. "Breakaway roping's next."

"Didn't you listen to the announcement?"

The rancher's nephew frowned. "Who does?"

"They've switched the calf roping and barrel race around."

"Yeah," Hip added. "Guess they were having some trouble getting the calves into the holding pen so they decided to give themselves a little more time."

Frank's cheeks paled and a strange, haunted look gleamed in his eyes. "Don't try to pull that on me!" he protested. "I know better."

"Listen and you'll find out," Greg said.

". . . The first rider in the girls' barrel race is 12-year-old Kimberly Powell. Good luck, Kim!"

She leaned low over the quarter horse's back and kicked Patches in the flanks with her heels. He leaped to a dead run.

"No!" Frank cried, waving his arms and dashing forward. "No!"

By this time she was galloping Patches at top speed, a smooth, effortless ride that looked deceptively easy, as though anyone who had ever been on a horse could do well in the barrel race. Greg was thrilled by the way she handled

Patches as she crossed the starting line and dashed for the first barrel. It was going to be a good run, he told himself. A very good run.

It was obvious that she didn't notice Frank at first, she was so intently concentrating on the first barrel. Then he must have come into focus. Frantically she jerked on one rein and Patches lurched to one side in a desperate attempt to follow her command. The surge of her weight, slight as it was, tore at the cinch. The strands parted and she pitched forward, her body hitting Frank in the chest like a missile out of a catapult. They went down together.

Pandemonium broke loose. People surged into the arena, crowding around the kids who were lying motionless on the ground. Greg and Hip were among the first to reach them with George, Christine and Kevin Powell only half a step behind. Lee Huffman and his wife arrived at about the same time, as did Dr. Lambert who had come out to the Lazy H to watch his son ride.

Christine Powell ran her hand gently over her daughter's white, drawn face, saying her name over and over again. The Huffmans tried to determine whether Frank was hurt. Dr. Lambert went to Kim first, determining hurriedly that she was shaken but not injured. Then he directed his attention to the boy on the ground beside her. Frank was groaning softly, his lips scarcely parting, and his arm was twisted grotesquely under him.

"Frank," the doctor said, his voice even and reassuring.

"My—my arm . . . it hurts!"

"Here, let me help you turn just a little so I can get a better look at it." He did so and the boy screamed with pain.

"It's broken, ain't it, Doc?" Lee Huffman demanded coarsely.

"I'm afraid so."

"It's broken all right," Mr. Huffman repeated. "I've seen too many broken bones not to recognize one."

The doctor nodded. "There's no doubt about it. It's broken. But we won't know how badly until we get him in to the hospital and take some X rays. Go in and call my office, Lee," he said. "Have Edith phone for the ambulance to come out and pick Frank up. Then tell her to call the hospital and have them get a room ready."

The ranch owner turned to one of the hands who was standing nearby. "You heard Doc. Get to that phone!"

Kim could not understand why Frank had done what he had and why she hadn't been hurt.

"It doesn't make sense," she told her parents, and Greg and Hip. "He came charging out in the arena, right in my path! If I hadn't jerked Patches to one side I—I'd have run right over him."

"When I saw you fall off," her mother said, her voice still trembling with emotion, "I was sure you were going to be badly hurt."

Kim paused. "I didn't fall off," she protested. "The cinch broke and the saddle came off."

"Whatever," Mrs. Powell said. "The important thing is that you and Frank weren't hurt seriously."

Greg and Hip watched while the doctor directed two men on making a stretcher with their coats and carrying the boy into the house out of the wind and the flaming sun.

"I sure hope Frank's arm isn't hurt too bad," Hip said.

"Me too."

"What do you suppose caused him to do what he did? I've never seen anything so stupid."

"Neither have I—unless . . ." Greg's voice trailed away.

"Unless what?"

"I want to take a look at something." Greg motioned his pal to follow. They went over to the saddle that was still on the hard ground where it had been thrown when it came off Patches.

Greg knelt beside it, examining the cinch carefully.

"Look!" he exclaimed, holding up the gray cinch. "Just as I thought!"

"It was cut!"

"Right on! That was intended for me. I was supposed to ride Patches in the breakaway roping but they switched the events and he got Kim instead."

Hip could scarcely believe that could be true. "Surely he wouldn't have done a thing like that!"

"The cinch was cut," Greg affirmed. "You can see that for yourself. And I saw Frank foolin' with Patches when Kim and I were coming back to the end of the arena where I'd tied him. I looked things over after he left but I guess I didn't look hard enough."

"I know he threatened to get even with you, but—"

"Look how that cinch was cut—from the inside next to the horse's belly so it wouldn't be seen. It had to be deliberate. There's no other explanation!"

Hipolita straightened and pulled in a deep breath. "I guess you're right, but I hate to think he's that kind of a guy."

"We'd just as well face it. That's exactly what he is. And I've got my doubts that he'll ever be any different."

Hip was very much concerned. "I guess that is the sort of thing that can happen when a guy isn't a believer," he said. "It's too bad we couldn't have reached him for Christ when we first met him. An awful lot of trouble would've been saved."

"Yeah." Greg felt the barb prick his heart. He had prayed for Frank regularly ever since he met him that first time at the Lazy H. He had even made a point of asking the family to pray for Frank, too. But deep in his heart he knew that he hadn't been all that concerned about his new friend. For all the praying he had done, he wondered now if he had honestly wanted Frank to receive Christ. He would have argued the question with anyone else; he tried to do the same with himself, but that was impossible. He recognized the reluctance in his own heart for what it was.

"What are you going to do?" Hip asked.

"Take the cinch to town and show it to him," he whispered.

His friend nodded and Greg took that to mean that Hip agreed with his decision.

He found a heavy paper bag in the trash barrel and put the cinch in it. He then stored it in the front of the trailer, out of reach of their horses' hooves.

They wanted to go to the hospital that afternoon but got back into Concord so late they had to wait until after supper. Greg wanted to tell his folks about the cut cinch, especially when they persisted in talking about how brave Frank had been. But he didn't dare.

"Don't forget," he did tell them, "he caused the accident in the first place."

"Maybe he did," Mr. Powell said. "But maybe he saw Kim's saddle slipping and sensed what was happening. We have to admit that he did keep Kimberly from getting hurt, at his own expense."

Hip came over as soon as he finished eating that night and the two boys walked to the hospital together. Kim wanted to go along, but Greg talked her out of it by suggesting that it would be better for her to see Frank the following afternoon when he was feeling better.

"All right," she said with obvious reluctance, "but I don't want him to think that I don't appreciate what he did for me."

Greg scowled but said nothing.

14.

Bernard Palmer

When Hip and Greg got to the hospital Frank was lying with his eyes closed and they thought he was asleep.

"Maybe we'd better come back later," Hip said.

At the sound of Hip's voice the injured boy looked up at him. "Hi," he said weakly.

"How're things going?" Greg wanted to know.

His face twisted into a weak smile. "In low gear right now."

"You don't look like you'll be riding old Blaze for a couple of days," Hip put in.

Frank's smile faded and for an instant he grimaced with pain. When he could speak again his voice was low, but edged with anger. "I don't know what difference it makes whether I've got a broken arm or not," he muttered, feeling very sorry for himself it seemed to Greg. "Uncle Lee won't let me ride any more. The truth is, he won't let me do nothin'."

A long, painful silence stood like a wall between them. Greg eyed the boy in bed uncomfortably. He should be talking to him, he knew, but what could he say?

Then Frank spied the sack Greg was carrying. "What you got there?" he asked curiously, as though he expected a gift or something.

Greg Powell winced. For the first time since they had entered the room he remembered the cut cinch he was carrying in the sack. He had brought it along, determined to throw it on the bed and demand an explanation. He and Frank were going to have a showdown and this time he knew who would be coming out on top.

Until now he had not realized the arrogance and lack of compassion in his plan to confront Frank this way. The other boy had only been in the hospital three or four hours and must be in terrible pain. His arm wouldn't even be set until the next day. Yet Greg had come to rip into him for what he had done. He hadn't even had the decency to wait until Frank was feeling better. Shame swept over him in waves.

"What you got there?" Frank persisted.

"Nothing that would interest you," he said lamely.

"How do you know?" Frank demanded. "Let me see."

Greg stepped back from the bed and shifted the bag from one hand to the other uncertainly. "I suppose you're going to take it away from me if I don't show it to you."

The rancher's nephew laughed.

"It's just something that belongs to me," Greg replied. "I shouldn't even have brought it along."

A strange fear twisted the injured boy's face and he lay back on the pillow and closed his eyes.

While Greg was still trying to think of something else to say to change the subject, the boys heard the crisp, businesslike footsteps of the doctor and his nurse in the hall outside the room.

"Hello, Frank," Dr. Lambert said cheerily. "How's the wing?"

"If you really want to know, it hurts bad."

"We just got your X rays. It's a nice, clean break. I don't anticipate any complications when we set it in the morning. You should be able to go home in a day or two."

At that moment he seemed to become aware of Greg and Hip. "Would you guys wait out in the hall a few minutes?" he asked.

"We'll see you tomorrow afternoon, Frank," Hip said.

"Oh, don't leave," the doctor protested. "We're just going to give him another shot for pain and put some more ice on his arm. We'll be finished in here in five minutes."

The boys went back to the waiting room where Greg left the sack on the hat rack.

"Aren't you going to talk to him about it tonight?" his companion wanted to know.

Greg shook his head.

After a few minutes they sauntered back down the hall to Frank's room. The doctor and nurse were just finishing. "I understand you're a real hero now," Dr. Lambert was saying to Frank.

"What do you mean?"

"I wasn't where I could see what happened, but others have told me that you saw Kim's saddle slipping and guessed that she was in trouble. That was why you ran out the way you did. It takes a brave person to do something like that."

The boy said nothing.

"You saved her a nasty injury, Frank. If you hadn't broken her fall, she could have been badly hurt."

"I ... I ..." He moistened his lips as though he wanted to say more but the words would not come out.

The doctor and his nurse left after a moment or two and the boys went back into the room.

"Now," Frank said, as soon as he saw them, "what've you got in that sack?"

"It—it's out in the waiting room," Greg told him defensively.

"Go after it. We'd just as well get this over with!"

Greg Powell shook his head. He could tell by Frank's remark that he knew what the sack contained.

"I—" he began.

But at that instant his dad and Mr. Huffman came in.

"I just talked to the doctor," the rancher said, pulling up a chair and sitting down beside the bed. "You're coming along great."

Frank nodded.

"There's something I've got to talk to you about," Mr. Huffman began. "I was going to wait until you're released but the doctor said it would be all right to talk to you now."

Frank's small features darkened. "Have Greg and Hip been talkin' to you?"

"This doesn't have anything to do with Greg

and Hip. It has to do with you and me."

"We'll go!" Greg said quickly. In fact he was anxious to get out of there.

But the rancher stopped him. "No way. I think you boys ought to hear this. . . ." He breathed deeply. "I owe you an apology, Frank."

"How come?" He was still suspicious.

"I kept liquor in the house and drank it myself. It was a great temptation to you, especially when you were concerned about your parents getting a divorce. I'm responsible for your drinking. Will you forgive me?"

Frank hesitated. "I—I—Uncle Lee, you didn't get me started drinking," he blurted. "I snitched wine and beer from Dad for two or three years before I came out here . . . so it wasn't your fault."

"But I had it available so it was easy for you to keep on." He paused for a moment or two. "I know that all the kids your age who get started drinking don't have it around the house, but when it's there the temptation is a lot greater."

He glanced up at George Powell who nodded gravely.

"Before I left to come to town this evening I asked your Aunt Florence to throw out all the liquor in the house. I'm through with that stuff."

For a time he looked beyond his nephew, the words caught in his throat. "And there's another thing I'm sorry for. I saw Greg and Hip and Kim and what nice kids they are and I wanted you to be like them, so I hauled you into town every Sunday so you could go to Sunday school and church. But your aunt and I didn't go ourselves. That's going to change from now on. Beginning in the morning, we're going to be there." He straightened slowly.

"I don't know much about this business of being a Christian, but I'm going to find out."

George Powell smiled. "That's good news, Lee."

"I'm not makin' any promises, mind you, but Florence and I have decided to see what it's all about."

"You'll never be sorry."

Mr. Huffman turned back to Frank. "I know it has been tough on you having your parents divorced and being forced to move out here with us, but we want to be your mom and dad from now on. OK?"

Frank took his uncle's hand with his own uninjured fingers and squeezed it affectionately.

Greg was sure that no one else could ever take the place of his own parents and he figured that was true of Frank, too. But living with someone like Lee and Florence Huffman, who loved him, would sure help.

After a time the two men left and Greg and Hip were alone in the room with Frank again. "I'm so thankful about your uncle," Hip said. "He'll be a Christian before long."

"Me too," Greg added. The silence was long and painful. Mr. Huffman had confessed to his nephew and he wasn't even a Christian. Greg knew that he had some confessing to do too. It wasn't going to be easy, but that didn't make any difference.

"I—I'm sorry for the way I treated you, Frank," he said.

"I deserved it," the other boy muttered. "I cut the cinch on your saddle so I could get back at you. But I wanted to get *you* hurt, not Kim."

Greg knew that but he said nothing about it. "That's all over and done with now."

"Then why did you bring the cinch out here in that sack?" Frank demanded belligerently.

Greg's cheeks flushed. "Because I was stupid, that's why. I shouldn't have done that—especially while you're in the hospital."

The corners of Frank's mouth tightened, but he did not reply.

"I've got something else to confess to you," Greg continued. "We prayed for you at home. I think we prayed for you every night."

"What's so bad about that?"

Greg hesitated momentarily. "That isn't what I meant," he said. "I prayed for you but I didn't really have the concern for you that I should have had. I said I wanted you to confess your sin and receive Christ as your Saviour, but I—I didn't care enough to share Christ with you."

"You talked with me about being a Christian," Frank told him.

"Maybe I did—once or twice—but I should have done more—a lot more. I was afraid of having you and your pals make fun of me, so I kept quiet mostly. If I'd been as concerned about you as I should have been, that fear wouldn't have made any difference." His gaze met Frank's. "Will you forgive me?"

The silence between them was electric. A nurse came in to bring Frank a pill. Not until she left did either of the boys say any more.

"Sure I'll forgive you, Greg," he said softly. For the space of a minute or more he looked beyond his visitor at the open door. "You might even talk to me about Christ now, if you want to," he said. "I—I'm sort of like Uncle Lee. I'm not making any promises, but I—I'd like to hear what you've got to say."

Eagerly Greg sat down beside the bed and began to explain the way of salvation. He told Frank that everyone is born a sinner and does bad things that make him deserve to go to hell, but that God provided a way of escape. That He sent His only Son to bring salvation to those who repented of the way they lived, confessed their sin and put their trust in Christ to save them. He quoted Bible verses to show his friend that what he was saying was true.

Frank listened intently and before Greg had half finished he knew that the rancher's nephew was going to become a believer. It might not happen that night but it would happen soon.

There was a song in his heart as he continued to tell Frank what the Bible said about being born again.

DATE DUE

772

OPEN DOOR BAPTIST CHURCH
PH: (403) 639-4994
P.O. BOX 1813
GRAND CENTRE, AB. T0A 1T0